#15

JUNIOR
HIGH

THE NIGHT
THE EIGHTH GRADE
RAN THE MALL

JUNIOR HIGH

#15

JUNIOR HIGH

THE NIGHT THE EIGHTH GRADE RAN THE MALL

Kate Kenyon

SCHOLASTIC INC.
New York Toronto London Auckland Sydney

No part of this publication may be reproduced in whole or in part, or stored in a retrieval system, or transmitted in any form or by any means, electronic, mechanical, photocopying, recording, or otherwise, without written permission of the publisher. For information regarding permission, write to Scholastic Inc., 730 Broadway, New York, NY 10003.

ISBN 0-590-42029-1

Copyright © 1989 by Ann Reit. All rights reserved. Published by Scholastic Inc. JUNIOR HIGH is a registered trademark of Scholastic Inc.

12 11 10 9 8 7 6 5 4 3 2 1   9/8 0 1 2 3 4/9

Printed in the U.S.A.   01

First Scholastic printing, April 1989

Chapter 1

They had pushed four tables together at the ice-cream parlor, Temptations, so they could all sit in one group. Something was happening in Cedar Groves that the eighth grade thought was absolutely going to change their lives. But before they could talk about it, they had to give their order to the waitress who was hovering next to the table.

"Come on, kids," she shouted over their voices. "Time for everyone to make up their minds. I haven't got all day for the ten-cent tip you'll probably leave for all eleven of you."

"Oh, Gloria, you know we're more generous than that," Jennifer Mann said. Under her joking there was a serious tone. Jennifer took care of the world: old people, whales, animals; and she couldn't stand the idea that Gloria really felt deprived of a decent tip.

Gloria smiled. "Okay, Jen, so you'll all leave a quarter. Now, what is everyone having? As if I didn't know. Nora, you'll have yogurt and probably sprinkle your own wheat germ on it. Never will you risk having anything not healthy. You probably think when you apply to medical school, they'll ask on the application if you've ever eaten anything loaded with non-nutritious goodies."

Nora took her ambition to be a doctor very seriously and couldn't really join in with the laughter that went around the table. "There's nothing wrong with eating decent, healthy food," she mumbled.

Jen came to the defense of Nora, who was her best friend since kindergarten. "Don't laugh at her. She's entitled to eat whatever she wants."

Steve Crowley, who thought Jen was the most wonderful girl in all of Cedar Groves Junior High, immediately said, "Yeah. She's right."

"Right about what, Steve?" Tracy asked, pushing her long blonde hair off her face. She had her Tracy-Douglas-puzzled look on her face; a look that just seemed to come naturally to her.

"Yeah, Steve," Tommy said, as he combed his sandy-brown hair for the fourteenth time that day. "Is Jen right because Nora is entitled to eat what she wants? Or is Nora right that there is nothing wrong with healthy foods?" Tommy looked around the table, waiting to see if the girls would all appreciate what he considered to be his sharp sense of humor.

Gloria held up her pad with a warning gesture. "*First*, we are going to talk about what everyone is ordering. Now!"

"Coke!"

"Chocolate ice cream!"

"Apple juice!"

"Blueberry pie!"

"Iced tea!"

"Cornflakes!"

"Wait a minute," Tommy yelled. "*Who* ordered cornflakes?"

"I did," Jason Anthony said, his fair eyebrows going up toward his red hair. "What's wrong with that?"

"Okay, okay," Gloria said. "Let's just finish this up without analyzing what everyone is eating."

When the orders had all been given, she left the table, shaking her head.

* * *

As soon as Gloria returned with the orders, and everyone had had a chance to sample theirs, Tracy began, "I want to talk about the *pool*."

"Tracy is right," Jen said. "It's the most incredible thing in the whole world. Cedar Groves is going to build a swimming pool! Can you believe it?"

Denise Hendrix smiled a slightly superior smile. "Well, don't expect it to be the most wonderful pool in this country. It will probably be a little rinky-dink." She smoothed back her shining blonde hair and refastened the real gold barrette that held it in place.

Denise Hendrix's father owned Denise Cosmetics, and the Hendrix family was rich. Denise had lived all over the world and had gone to a private school in Switzerland before Mr. Hendrix had moved his family back to his hometown, Cedar Groves. Denise was a year older than the other girls, and though she really tried to fit in with the other eighth-graders, she sometimes couldn't help letting them know she was really much more sophisticated than they were.

"I'll probably be the only one to put it to good use," Mitch Pauley said. "You have to be an athlete, like me, to really know how to make the most of a swimming pool."

4

"Mitch, keep quiet," Susan said.

Nora held up a hand commandingly. "You're all jumping ahead way too fast. Cedar Groves can't build the pool until they have the money. Remember?"

Mia Stevens stopped pulling at the pink spikes in her punk hairstyle and said, "Well, they have half the money. I mean, the city treasury is going to provide half the amount needed. Right?"

"Yeah," Steve said. "And the rest of the city is going to raise the other half. That includes all of us, our parents, the school, businesses, etc., etc., etc."

"I say let the etceteras raise the rest, and we'll just wait to swim in the pool," Jason said.

"That's what you call civic spirit," Lucy Armanson answered, smoothing down the turtleneck on her chic yellow sweater, and running her fingers through her short Afro.

Jason shrugged. "How are kids like us supposed to raise money? I mean, *real* money. It's nuts."

"Well," Tommy said, grinning. "*You* could start by selling your skateboard. You'd get at least four cents for that."

"Sell my skateboard! I'd rather not have the pool," Jason said.

"He means that," Nora said. "Can you believe it?"

"Look," Steve said, "we're all intelligent human beings. We should be able to come up with a way to raise some money."

"I don't think Jason is either intelligent or human," Susan said.

"Can we just not argue?" Jen shouted. "We have a real problem here. Do you want the pool or not? Think how wonderful it would be on warm summer days to just lie around a gorgeous pool . . . with all our friends." She looked at Steve as she talked, and blushed slightly.

Steve gazed back at Jen. "Yeah," he whispered to her, looking into her hazel eyes.

"Okay," Nora said. "So, all we have to do is figure out how we can raise some money."

"We can have a dance party benefit," Mia said, standing up and dancing around the table.

"Where?" Tommy asked.

"Oh, don't be so worried about *details*," Mia answered.

"Sure, sure," Mitch said. "That's just a *small* detail. Where to have it. Mia, you're a flake."

"We could have a contest," Jason said. "For the most beautiful skateboard in Cedar Groves."

"He's bonkers." Susan sneered. "I always knew it."

"We could make and sell healthy, vegetarian, unpreserved meals," Nora said.

Everyone made retching noises.

"Okay. Okay," Nora said.

Jen stood up and put her hands on her hips. "Look, everyone is just throwing out dumb, spur-of-the-moment ideas that don't make any sense."

"Thanks a bunch," Nora muttered.

"Jen is right," Denise said. "We are talking about real money here, not nickels and dimes. Four dollars isn't going to help us get much of a pool."

Steve looked up at Jen and smiled. "I agree with Jen."

Tracy sighed. "You *always* agree with Jen. I wish I had a boy who agreed with *me*."

"You just wish you had a boy," Susan said.

"We can always count on you to say something nice, Susan," Mitch said.

Lucy banged her fist on the table and said, "This is ridiculous. We are all bickering and getting no place. I suggest we all think tonight, seriously and carefully, about a good way to raise money. We can meet tomorrow and talk about our ideas."

"I second the motion," Tracy said.

"No one made a motion," Steve said.

"Well, it sounded like a motion to me."

"Okay. Okay." Denise stood up and gathered her books together. "Let's meet at my house after school tomorrow. I have the most space to handle this mob."

"I second the motion," Tracy said.

Chapter 2

That night, as always, Jen and Nora spoke on the phone. Jen had been writing in her diary when Nora called, and she put the blue leather book on the table next to her bed. She lifted up the pink princess phone and said, "Hi, Nora."

"How did you know it was me? It could have been Kirk Cameron or someone from U2 or even Steve!"

Jen laughed. "Steve called already. And I'm not expecting Kirk or anyone of the 2s to call tonight."

"Have you thought of anything yet?" Nora asked.

"Not really," Jen answered, straightening the white chenille bedspread on her bed. She knew that Jeff, their beloved and loving housekeeper, hated her to sit on the white spread, but Jen always felt if you weren't supposed to sit on the bed, then there shouldn't be a phone next to it.

"Me, neither," Nora said.

"Well, I do my best thinking after I've turned out the lights, so I have time to come up with a master plan."

"Ho ho," Nora said. "You sound sure of yourself."

"Well, I'm not. Listen, what are you going to wear tomorrow?"

That was always part of their nightly call . . . they planned what they would wear the next day.

"*That* I am sure of," Jen said. "My green bulky sweater and the gray denims."

"Okay. I guess I'll wear my new tights, the red mini, and the red-and-white striped sweatshirt."

"You'll look like a peppermint stick," Jen said.

"I should be that skinny. See you tomorrow."

As Jen hung up, there was a knock on her door. "Can I come in?" her father's voice called out.

"Sure," Jen replied. She liked it when her father came in at night and sat on the edge of her bed, and they could talk privately. She knew that he did it partly because he liked it, too, and partly because he felt that it would make up a little for her mother, who had died when Jen was very young. Jen knew he was sure her mother would have come in every night, if she had been alive.

Jen could hardly remember her mother. Maybe the scent of her perfume; the way her voice sounded something like little bells; the way she laughed. But Jen knew that her father still missed her very much. Sometimes Jen thought that Ted Mann should get married again . . . though the idea scared her. Just the way the idea that Jeff might someday marry his girlfriend, Debby Kincaid, and leave the Manns, frightened her. Jeff had been their housekeeper for years, and the thought of his not being with them was something Jen pushed away.

"How was school today?" her father asked. "Somehow, dinners are always so frantic I never feel we have a chance to catch up. Your brother, Eric, takes up so much talk-time at the table, that you seem to get short shrift."

Jen laughed and put her cheek against her father's shoulder. "Don't worry, Dad, I don't feel neglected. Actually, the most interesting part of school was after school. The gang tried to think of some ways to come up with money for the pool."

"And . . ." her father said.

"And nothing. We decided to think about it and all meet at Denise's tomorrow to discuss our brilliant thoughts. Of which, so far, I have none."

Mr. Mann nodded. "I know. We were talking about the same thing in the office today. Although, I must admit, the idea of all you kids cavorting in the pool makes me uneasy."

"Dad, you are really such a worrier. There will be a lifeguard, you know."

Mr. Mann laughed, patted Jen's cheek, and pushed her long dark hair off her forehead. "I guess I worry for two." He leaned over and kissed Jen. "Good-night, sweetheart."

Jen turned off the light next to her bed and snuggled under the covers. Where, she thought, could they make money?

The next day after school, they all gathered at Denise's. The Hendrixes' house was so big and sprawling that it held the eighth-graders easily. Betty, the Hendrixes' maid, had set up cold drinks and cookies in the den, and everyone descended on them immediately. Betty stood back as they surrounded the table and said, "Easy, kids. Don't shove, spill, or break. There *is* more where all that came from."

When everyone had something to eat, Denise

said, "Okay. So who has some useful thoughts?"

"Well, Andy and I could make a tape of some of our music and sell it," Mia said proudly.

Mitch hooted. "Yeah, and the only people who will buy it are *your* parents."

"I could do a skateboard exhibition and sell tickets," Jason said.

"Even your *parents* wouldn't come to that," Susan said.

"I still think some kind of nonpreserved cookie would sell," Nora said.

"I don't think so, Nora," Jen said gently.

"We girls could put on a fashion show," Denise said.

"Boy, *that's* sure fascinating," Tommy said. "I can't wait to buy tickets for *that*."

"So what is *your* great idea?" Denise asked with annoyance.

"How about if the *boys* put on a fashion show?" Tommy asked, running a comb through his hair.

"Yeah," Susan said. "You'd all be perfect examples of what the well-dressed man *shouldn't* wear."

Everyone glared at each other silently.

Finally, Jen said, "Look, we have to figure out where people spend their money and on what."

"No problem," Steve answered. "They spend their money at the mall . . . and they spend it on everything there."

The group all thought about that for a few moments.

Then Jen said, "Okay, then we have to think of something to do at the mall."

"We have to sell something there, obviously," Tracy said. "But what?"

Mitch hooted again. "What do we do, just set up a lemonade stand in the middle of the mall? There are even laws against that, I bet."

Lucy looked down at her prefectly pressed green pants and then said, "What if we could get whatever permit we need to sell at the mall?"

Nora shrugged. "Then we are left with a permit, and we still don't have any ideas of what to sell that anyone would want to buy."

Jen hesitated. Then she said, "This may sound crazy, but what if some of the shop owners let us sell *their* stuff?"

"What do you mean?" Tracy asked. "And even if you know what you mean, why would they let us do that?"

"What *do* you mean?" Nora asked.

"Well," Jen said, gathering enthusiasm. "What if they let us run their stores for one night?"

Steve frowned. "Jen, what storeowner in his or her right mind is going to let us do that?"

"And what kind of a store could *I* run?" Tracy asked.

"Look," Jen said. "I'm talking about a few hours. Say from five to eight one night and whatever money we make goes to the pool fund."

Susan shook her head in disgust. "That whole idea is nuts. Why would the owners just give away bunches of money?"

"Because they are supposed to raise money for the pool, too. So a scheme like Jen's would make it seem like they are cooperating," Steve said. "And . . . if we split what we make with the owners, they'd come out ahead, too."

"They *would* get a lot of publicity," Lucy said. "Everyone in the city would know what they were doing."

"Right," Jen said. "And everyone would come into the stores to see us and buy from us. It's a wonderful idea . . . if I do say so myself."

Nora looked skeptical. "I don't know. I just don't see this at all."

"Me, neither," Tommy said.

"I don't get it," Mitch agreed.

"Why don't we just go ask a couple of store-owners in the mall and see what they say?" Tracy asked.

The group was silent for a moment.

"She's right," Steve said. "That's the logical thing to do."

"She's never right," Susan said.

"That's where *you're* wrong," Lucy said.

"Okay," Denise shouted. "I don't really see this as working, either, but I agree with Tracy, let's go ask someone. Tomorrow after school."

"Who do we go to?" Tracy asked.

"Well, I buy a lot of stuff at the Chic Boutique," said Denise. "Let's start there. At least they'll let us in."

"Okay," Jen said. "Tomorrow after school. But we can't all go in together. We'll terrify the owner. Denise, you go, since they know you. And Lucy, you're so chic, you go with her. Okay?"

"Fine," Denise said. "But I don't hold out much hope."

"It can't hurt to try," Lucy said. "We'll meet after school tomorrow and see what the Chic Boutique says. You have to have a positive point of view, Denise."

"Okay," Denise said, "I'll be positive, but . . . I *still* don't hold out much hope."

Chapter 3

The next day, Denise and Lucy stood outside of the Chic Boutique at the Twin Rivers Mall and looked at each other nervously. They had both, without even discussing it, dressed in their newest, most stylish clothes. Now, Denise clutched Lucy's hand and said, "What are we nervous about? We certainly have a right to go in and talk about the plans for raising money for the pool. Don't we?"

"Of course," Lucy said. "But let's go and get it over with."

As soon as they stepped inside the shop, the owner, Ms. Garston, came over to Denise. "Denise, it's so good to see you. In fact, I got a leather skirt in yesterday, and as soon as I saw it I thought to myself, *that* is for Denise Hendrix."

"Um," Denise said slowly. "This is my friend Lucy Armanson."

Ms. Garston smiled at Lucy. "So nice to meet you. Is there anything in particular you'd like to see?"

"Not exactly," Lucy said, as slowly as Denise had.

"You see, Ms. Garston, we aren't really here to buy anything," Denise said.

"Oh," the shop owner said. "Just to browse? Well, feel free."

Denise cleared her throat. "We aren't here to browse, either."

Ms. Garston looked at the two girls. "Oh, I know, you need to use the bathroom. Well, go right ahead. Denise, you know where it is."

"That isn't it, either," Lucy said.

Ms. Garston smiled. "Okay, *you* tell me. Why are you here?"

"Well," Denise said. "It's about raising money for the pool."

"Of course I'm going to contribute to the pool fund, Denise. The store owners in the mall thought we should all make one joint contribution."

Denise and Lucy exchanged a look.

Then Denise just took a deep breath and rushed into her story. "You see, Ms. Garston, we eighth-graders want to contribute, too, and we thought if the store owners at the Twin Rivers Mall would allow us to run their stores for one night, we could raise a lot of money, split the money with the owner, and give the rest to the pool fund, and think of all the publicity you would get by letting us do this."

"Wait, Denise! You mean you want me to let you run *this* store for a night?" Ms. Garston looked a little pale.

"Not a whole night," Denise said. "Just a few hours . . . from, say, five to eight. I could do it and Lucy could, too, and it would raise a lot of money. I know it. Everyone in town would come to the mall to watch the kids running things."

Ms. Garston sank into a small chair nearby and said faintly, "Denise, you don't know anything about running a store."

Denise knelt next to the chair. "It's just for a few hours. I can sell clothes. And if anything went wrong, we would call you to come right over. Think of how cooperative and civic-minded everyone would think you were."

"Have you spoken to other store owners in the mall? What do they think of this scheme?" Ms. Garston asked.

Denise sighed. "Well, actually, you're the first one we've spoken to."

"I don't know, Denise. If it weren't *my* store,

I'd say it's an original idea. And you're right, it *would* attract a lot of people down here. But . . . you have no experience. Who knows what might happen?"

Denise stood up and said eagerly, "What could happen? You know me. I would take good care of your merchandise, and Lucy is even more responsible than I am."

Ms. Garston smiled. "I'll tell you what. If you can get other store owners to agree to this idea, I'll go along with it, too. But I won't be the only one."

Denise gave the woman a hug. "I know we'll get other people to agree. I know it. I'll let you know who as soon as possible."

Outside the store, the girls threw their arms around one another. "I'm sure she'll do it," Lucy said. "All we have to do is get some other places to go along with it."

Denise kept an arm around Lucy as they walked. "I'll call all the kids tonight and we'll get together after school tomorrow and work out where we go from here."

"We can meet at my house tomorrow," Lucy said.

They all piled into Lucy's living room the next afternoon and listened to Lucy and Denise's report eagerly.

"Okay," Nora said. "I don't believe this, but the next step is to figure out what other places we want to hit and who should go."

"One thing is certain," Mia said, "Andy and I go to the Record Mart. We're naturals for it."

No one could argue about that, but Jen said hesitantly, "Could you both dress just a little more carefully? I mean, could you have your hair a real hair color? After all, you *are* going to be asking people to take a big chance on you. And the more, well, mature, you look. . . ."

"I get your point, Jen," Mia said with visible annoyance.

"Obviously," Steve said, "I should go to the Burger Barn. I know a lot about food from the time I spend in my father's restaurant."

"I'll go with Steve," Jen said quickly.

"Great," Steve said, smiling warmly at Jen. It still amazed him that this girl he had known since kindergarten was suddenly a special girl to him . . . not just a friend, but a girl he thought of first thing in the morning and the last thing at night.

"I want to go to the Clip 'N' Curl," Tracy said. "I love anything to do with hair." She stroked her shining, long blonde hair.

"I'll go with Tracy," Nora said. "After what

they did to my hair recently, they owe me a favor."

"I want the Mall Cinema," Jason said. "What could be better than running a movie theater?"

"I don't trust Jason to do *anything* right," Susan said immediately. "I'll go with him and make sure he doesn't send the theater into bankruptcy in three hours."

"Well, there's no doubt where I'm going," Mitch said. "Norton's Sporting Goods."

"I'll go there, too," Tommy said.

"You're no athlete," Mitch said.

"Yeah, but girls probably think it's a real masculine thing to be doing . . . working in a sporting goods place. It's good for my image."

"Okay," Lucy said. "So tomorrow after school you all have to talk to the owners and convince them to go along with our idea. You have to seem responsible and mature and capable . . . just like Denise and I did."

Susan looked annoyed. "I assure you, anything that you and Denise can do, *I* can do. In spite of Jason."

Right after school the next day, the group met on the steps of the junior high and gave each other last-minute instructions.

"Jason, leave the skateboard here!"

"Mia, can't you make your skirt a little longer?"

"Susan, try to look pleasant. Just for once."

"Tommy, get your mind off girls for just a little while."

"Nora, put the carrots away."

They all made faces at one another and took off.

Mia and her boyfriend, Andy Warwick, approached the Record Mart, and Mia tried to push down the spikes in Andy's hair. "I never realized that it stood up *that* high."

Andy pushed her hand away. "You should talk. Pink is *not* a normal color for hair."

"Okay. Okay," Mia said. "Let's not argue."

Inside the store, the owner came over to them right away. "Hi, kids. What do you want today?"

Mia cleared her throat. "Hi, Mr. Paley. We have something we want to talk to you about."

Quickly, before she lost her nerve, Mia told the owner what she wanted.

Mr. Paley took a few steps backward, away from Mia and Andy. "You *have* to be kidding. I can't do that."

Mia put her hand on his arm. "You know we know everything about records."

Mr. Paley patted Mia's hand gently. "Sure you know everything about records — and nothing about running a store. Do you know how to detect shoplifters? How to work the computer? How to keep track of exactly what you sell?"

Andy looked upset. "Not exactly, but — "

Mia interrupted impatiently. "We can learn. We'll do fine."

Mr. Pauley laughed. "Come back in five years. Then . . . maybe."

At the Mall Cinema, the manager, Pete Tabor, laughed out loud. "You have to be kidding. Let you kids run this theater, even for three hours? You're both nuts."

"Wait a minute, Mr. Tabor," Susan said angrily.

Jason shook his head at her. "*Don't* get angry," he muttered.

The manager started to laugh again, slapping his thigh. "Tell you what. I'll let you both in free today, just to make you feel better, but run this place . . . never."

"Free!" Jason shouted. "Great!"

Susan pulled on his arm. "Don't be ridiculous. Who needs his free admittance when he has just insulted us? We're leaving."

She pulled Jason out of the theater.

* * *

As Jen and Steve walked into the Burger Barn, the manager, Frank Yancy, walked over to them. "Hey, Steve. How's your dad? How's his restaurant doing?"

"Fine, Frank. Fine. You know I'm there a lot, too. I know everything about his business."

"Great, Stevie-boy. I'm sure someday you'll be a big help to him."

Jen cleared her throat, and before the manager and Steve got into a long discussion about restaurants, she told Frank Yancy why she and Steve were there.

Frank Yancy just shook his head. "First of all, this place is part of a chain. I can't make a decision like that. And even if I could, the answer would be no. Steve, you know better than to make a suggestion like this. You know what it takes to run a food place . . . and a fast-food restaurant is different than a place like your father's."

"Frank," Steve said, a pleading tone in his voice. "Jen and I are real responsible. We could do it."

"Sure we could," Jen said firmly.

"Well, kids," Frank Yancy said, "I'm not going to give you a chance to prove it in *my* place. Sorry."

* * *

At the beauty parlor, Nora and Tracy weren't having any better luck. There was a brand-new owner, Ms. Jacobs, who just looked at Tracy and said, "You need a haircut, and no, you can't run my shop, not for three minutes, let alone three hours."

Nora put one hand on her hip and ran her other hand through her curly brown hair. "You owe me a favor after what you did to my hair recently. Remember that permanent this place gave me? It made my hair look like a curly mop."

"Mistakes happen," Ms. Jacobs said, "and I'm sorry for that. But one mistake I won't make is letting kids run my shop."

Mitch and Tommy walked out of Norton's Sporting Goods store dejected. Tommy looked at Mitch scathingly. "I thought you said you and Mr. Norton were real pals. That he'd do anything for you."

Mitch shrugged. "I guess anything isn't really anything."

"He practically had hysterics, he laughed so hard," Tommy said.

"I told you he was a very cheerful guy," Mitch answered.

Tommy reached out and punched Mitch's arm. "You sure had the wrong idea about Mr. Norton."

"But he *is* cheerful, isn't he?"

Tommy just groaned.

Chapter 4

After they left the Burger Barn, Steve and Jen walked in silence. Steve held Jen's hand, and every now and then squeezed it reassuringly.

"We'll find a way to work this out. I know we will," he said, but he didn't sound very sure.

Jen tried to smile. "I guess. But how?"

Steve shrugged. "Let's go to my dad's restaurant. We'll get some nice, sweet dessert and talk."

As soon as they walked into the red, white, and black restaurant, Joe Crowley walked over to them. "You both look awful. What happened and what do you want to eat?"

They sat at a table and Jen and Steve asked for chocolate cake and milk. Jen told Mr. Crowley the whole story, and he looked thoughtful.

"What about the other stores? What happened there?" he asked.

"We don't know," Steve answered. "We haven't seen the other kids yet."

Joe Crowley sighed and smoothed out the red-and-white-checked tablecloth. "You can't really blame Frank. I mean . . . you're just kids. Inexperienced, too."

Steve bristled. "I've worked here a lot, and Jen works at the animal shelter, the senior citizens home, all kinds of places. That's experience."

"A different kind," Mr. Crowley said. The waiter brought the cake and milk, and Mr. Crowley said, "Eat up. You'll feel better."

"I'll eat up," Jen said, "but I won't feel better."

"It seems to me, if there's a chance at all that this will work out — and I'm still not sure it's a good idea, but I do admire you kids for thinking of it and trying — well, you have to do a few things first." Mr. Crowley stopped.

"Like what?" Steve asked.

"Well, it wouldn't hurt to let the newspaper know what you're doing. Let it get around that you have this scheme. That way the places in the mall will see they are getting instant publicity."

"Good thinking, Dad," Steve said.

"Parents *do* have good ideas once in a while," Joe Crowley said sarcastically.

"What else, Mr. Crowley?" Jen asked. "You said we have to do a few things."

"Well," Steve's father went on, "if a kid came in here with your idea, first I'd say no, right away, but then I might reconsider, if . . ."

"If what?" Steve asked impatiently.

"If *I* could make the rules for what the kid could and couldn't do," Mr. Crowley said. "If I could be assured by the kid that my rules would be obeyed and that the kid wouldn't run wild and just do whatever he or she wanted."

"That seems fair," Jen said eagerly. "It's certainly worth a try."

"First we have to find out what luck the rest of the gang had," Steve said. "Maybe their owners or managers were more reasonable than Frank."

"Want to bet?" Joe Crowley said. Then he stood up and went into the kitchen.

Steve finished the last drop of milk and pushed the glass away from him. He reached over and took Jen's hand. "I'm glad at least we're in this together. I mean, that we both are going to work at the Burger Barn, if we work anywhere at all."

Jen smiled. "Me, too," she said.

Steve looked around the empty restaurant and quickly leaned over and kissed Jen lightly.

"Whenever we're together it's fun," he whispered.

"I think so, too," she replied. Everything about Steve was special to her, from his wonderful blue eyes, to his dark brown hair, to his smile, to his intelligence. She still couldn't get over the fact that this boy, whom she had known all her life, was now a special boy.

The next morning, as always, the eighth grade gathered on the steps of Cedar Groves Junior High. The only cool thing to do, they all agreed, was stay outside until the bell rang, and then race into their homeroom.

"So what happened to all of you yesterday?" Jen asked.

They all admitted they had had absolutely no success.

"This idea just isn't going to work," Mitch said.

"Yeah, we're going to have to think of something else," Tommy agreed.

"Not me," Tracy said. "I've done all the thinking I'm going to do about this. We have to make the owners listen to us."

"They listen, all right," Jason said. "They just say no after they listen."

As the bell rang, Steve cried out, "Everyone

meet in the cafeteria for lunch. My father had some good ideas I want to tell you about."

"Your *father* had some good ideas?" Jason repeated.

"Yeah," Steve said. "Parents do have good ideas sometimes."

Jen snickered.

The eighth grade could hardly wait for lunchtime. They tried to concentrate on their classes, but one subject just ran into another until they all gathered around one huge table in the cafeteria. They were so eager to hear what Steve had to say that they hardly noticed the pea-green walls and the dingy linoleum floor.

As always, Nora brought a tray that held a salad, fruit, and a glass of milk. Jen bravely took the day's special and a piece of orange layer cake. Jason peered in everyone's food and stuck a finger into Susan's chocolate pudding. She slapped at his hand and a glob of the pudding flew onto Tracy's blouse.

"Look what you did," Tracy yelled at Jason.

"*Moi?* I didn't do anything. If Susan would keep her hands to herself, everything would be cool," Jason said.

"If you weren't such a pig . . ." Susan said.

Nora put her head in her hands. "Look, we came here to hear what Steve had to say. So could all of you just shut up, so he can talk?"

"Right," Jen said emphatically.

"It's simple," Steve said. "One: My father thinks we should tell the newspaper about our plan. And two: We should get the store owners and managers to outline what they would let us do and not do. That way they might feel more . . . comfortable about us sort of taking over."

"You mean, we have to go back and see them *again*?" Mia asked. "I don't know if I can take the humiliation."

"I think we should all do it together," Jen said. "Ask them if they would meet us all somewhere and we could negotiate as a group. In union there is strength," she said in a superior tone.

"We have to form a *union* to do this?" Tracy asked.

"No, Tracy. It's just an expression," Nora answered patiently.

"I don't know how much of this I can take," Susan put her hand to her forehead.

"Well, Susan, you could just leave and someone else can be in the Mall Cinema with Jason." Lucy smiled innocently.

"Yeah, Susan," Jason said quickly. "You could just leave and someone else can be in the Mall Cinema with me."

Susan glared at Lucy and Jason.

"Okay, so who is going to call the newspaper?" Andy Warwick asked. "I don't think they'll listen to me."

"You could try singing your message. Like a singing telegram," Mitch said, laughing.

"Then *certainly* no one will listen," Tommy said.

"My father knows the editor," Denise said, ignoring Tommy and Mitch. "I'll get him to call. But what do we want him to say?" As Denise spoke, the little silver bell earrings she was wearing tinkled softly.

"I'd kill for those earrings," Tracy said.

"I always knew there was a violent streak in her," Susan said.

Everyone laughed.

Denise bit her lip with annoyance. "I have never seen a group with a shorter attention span. Can't we try to stay on the same subject for more than two minutes?"

"Okay, okay," Nora said. "Just tell your father to ask the editor if he'll print a story about how we're trying to get some of the businesses in the mall to agree to have us run things for three hours to raise money for the swimming pool. It's simple."

Jason was on his feet, looking at the rice pudding on Lucy's tray. She put her hands over the dish and then lifted them. "On second consideration," Lucy said, "take it."

"That bad?" Jason asked. He sat down again.

"How are we going to get the owners to meet with us?" Steve asked. "That isn't going to be easy."

Jen smiled slyly. "We have to make them think *some* of the owners and managers are interested in our idea. Then they'll feel they have to at least consider it and meet us. Don't you think?"

"Brilliant," Steve said.

"Naturally," Susan muttered. "Jen said it."

"Well, it *is* brilliant," Nora said, beaming at Jen.

As the bell rang, Lucy shouted above the noise in the cafeteria. "Okay, we all have our jobs cut out for us. Denise gets her dad to call the newspaper and the rest of us go back to see the people in the mall."

Two days later, there was an article on the front page of the *Cedar Groves Herald* with a small headline, reading:

EIGHTH-GRADERS OFFER TO RUN THE
MALL TO RAISE MONEY FOR OUR POOL

The article told the whole story in a few paragraphs, ending with the statement that the students had so far been turned down by the owners and managers, but they were hoping to change the adults' minds.

The day before the article appeared, the group had gone to the stores in the mall again and had gotten the managers to agree to meet with the class the next day. And so, after school, the kids and the adults sat down together around a table in the corner of the Burger Barn.

Chapter 5

They sat in an uneasy silence for a little while. A big pot of coffee was in the center of the table for the adults, and the eighth-graders were drinking milk, soft drinks, and fruit juice.

Finally, Ms. Jacobs said, "Okay, we all know what we're here for, so let's get to the business at hand. Now, who is the idiot or who are the idiots who think this thing is a good idea?"

Jen's eyes widened and she and Nora exchanged a nervous look.

"Well," Jen said, "no one *exactly* agreed to this."

Frank Yancy looked at Steve. "But you said that one of the group was interested in this scheme."

"Well, you have to admit, everyone thinks the idea is *interesting*. Don't you?" Steve asked hesitantly.

"I think the idea is nuts," Mr. Paley of the Record Mart said.

"I agree," Mr. Tabor said, shaking his head. "You can come to my movie theater, kids, but don't run it."

All the owners made sounds of agreement with Mr. Paley.

Mr. Norton turned to Mitch. "You got us all here under false pretenses. I never would have come, if I hadn't thought someone else was going along with your plan." He started to get up from the table.

"Wait a minute, Paul," George Paley said, "we have another consideration here . . . the newspaper article."

"What's that got to do with anything?" Paul Norton asked, sitting down again.

"Well, Cedar Groves now knows that the kids have come up with this crazy idea. How will it look to the town if we refuse them?"

"It will look as if we're sane," Helen Garston said. "Who in their right minds would let a bunch of kids run their stores? Not my Chic Boutique."

"I want to know who is responsible for that article in the paper. Which of you kids put it there?" Frank Yancy asked.

"My father suggested it," Steve said.

"I don't believe it! I thought he was a friend of mine," Mr. Yancy said.

"And *my* father called the editor of the paper," Denise said proudly.

"*Your* father did a thing like that?" Tina Jacobs said.

"Yes," Denise answered. "I guess *he* doesn't think we're just a bunch of irresponsible kids."

"You must have twisted his arm," Pete Tabor said. "Bad."

Everyone began talking at once, yelling over each other. Finally, Nora yelled the loudest. "You have to admit, you already have a certain amount of publicity . . . and you'll get even more if you let us do this."

"She's right about the publicity," Mr. Norton said. "And I don't mind a certain amount of free promotion for my sporting goods. Business isn't that good that I can't use it."

Helen Garston refilled her coffee cup and said, "What worries me is, how will it look to Cedar Groves if we turn these kids down? Everyone knows about the idea. Won't we seem to be uncooperative if we say no?"

"That's a good point," Tina Jacobs said. "I can just see the newspaper headline: 'Mall Stores Refuse to Help Raise Money For Cedar Groves Pool.'"

The eighth-graders remained silent, knowing they were making progress. They just let the adults talk.

Pete Tabor wiped the sweat off his forehead. "Are you suggesting I let *kids* run my theater? Never!"

"Or my beauty parlor?"

"Or my record store?"

"Or this Burger Barn?"

Suddenly, Tracy interrupted. "Honestly, all this fuss over three hours, one night. We aren't asking to take over the mall. It's just three little hours."

"That's true," George Paley said. "It *is* just three hours. How much damage can they do in three hours?"

"Plenty," Paul Norton said.

"Look," Steve said, suddenly remembering what his father had said. "My father said you should give us rules for what we can and can't do in your stores. We won't do anything you don't agree to and we promise to obey whatever rules you make. That's fair, isn't it?"

The owners looked at each other, raising eyebrows, narrowing lips, drumming their fingers on the table.

"And," Jen said, excitedly, "the minute anything goes wrong . . . *if* anything goes wrong

. . . we will call you. You can rush right to your place and take over again."

"Right," Jason said.

"Good thinking," Lucy said.

"I'm with you," Nora said.

Helen Garston sighed loudly. "Nothing makes me feel really good about this . . . but I can't afford bad publicity. I don't want the town to think we won't do *anything* to help build the pool."

Mia looked at George Paley. "And whatever money we make . . . and we are bound to make pots . . . you all get half of it . . . without doing *anything*."

Mr. Paley rolled his eyes. "Nothing except risking our stores."

Andy frowned. "Mr. Paley, are there any other two kids in Cedar Groves who know more about music and records than Mia and me? Tell the truth."

"Andy," Mr. Paley said wearily, "I never said you and Mia didn't know a lot about the records themselves, it's all the other stuff you don't know."

"Look," Frank Yancy said, "I don't know if we have much choice. I'm with Helen; I can't risk getting all of Cedar Groves mad at me. I say we go along with the kids. We give them a list of rules. They promise to live up to them and to call us the second they have a problem."

"Okay, I'll go along with that, too," Pete Tabor said.

"Anyone who isn't going to agree to this, raise a hand," Mr. Yancy said.

Not one hand went up.

Steve jumped up and pulled Jen with him. They danced around the table. "Great," he shouted.

"You won't regret this," Nora said. "None of you."

"I doubt that," Tina Jacobs said. "I regret it already, and nothing has happened yet."

Paul Norton held up a hand to stop the eighth-graders from shouting and slapping each other on their backs. "Tomorrow, after school, you come to the store you are going to be responsible for and get the list of rules we will each have ready. You read them carefully. Memorize them. Promise to obey, etc., etc. Okay, class dismissed."

Outside, the eighth-graders hugged each other. Jason careened around on his skateboard. Mitch stood on his hands. Mia sang loudly.

"Okay," Nora said. "Tomorrow is Friday. Pick up the rules after school and everyone meet at my house tomorrow night so we can go over everything."

"I have a date with Timothy Marks tomorrow night," Denise complained.

"So break it for the good of Cedar Groves," Lucy said.

"We'd better make a lot of money," Denise grumbled.

"No doubt about that," Jen said happily.

"I hope so," Tracy muttered softly.

The next night, the group gathered around the big table in Nora's kitchen. In the center were bowls of potato chips and pretzels, soft drinks, and a huge platter of cookies that looked like they had been made of vegetables.

Nora pointed to the cookies. "Mine," she said with pride.

Nora's older sister Sally pointed to the rest of the things. "Mine," she said. Then she went back to doing graceful deep-knee bends to keep herself limber for the dancing classes she took. She was preparing for the ballet, but her diet, much to Nora's disgust, was at times as junky as anyone else's.

Tracy slapped Jason's hand as it went from bowl to bowl. "Leave something for the rest of us."

"I'm leaving Nora's cookies. What more do you want?"

Just then, Jessica Ryan, Nora's mother, came in and sat down at the table. Jen leaned over and whispered in Nora's ear, "Is your mother going to stay all night?"

Nora whispered back, "I think so. I can't help it. She'll explain."

Jessica Ryan then said, "I know how delighted you all are to have me here, but as you all know, I'm a lawyer. Now I think what you are about to do is admirable, but you could fall into all sorts of legal traps unless you do just what I say. First, I want each of you to read the instructions you were given this afternoon. Jen and Steve, you are going to the Burger Barn, right? Okay, Jen, read what Mr. Yancy wrote."

Jen cleared her throat and began. " 'One: You cannot, I repeat *cannot*, cook *anything*. Not even heat a bun. Two: You cannot go near any of the equipment. Three: You *can* clear off the tables and fill the ketchup and mustard containers. Four: You can amuse the children who come in. Five: You can get things for the girls and boys behind the counter. Six: You can help people, who need assistance or ask for assistance, to carry their trays.' "

"Okay, Jen," Mrs. Ryan said. "Is that clear? You keep away from cooking and stoves and anything that can break."

"He sure doesn't trust us," Steve said.

"It's okay, Steve," Jen said, patting his hand. "We'll do fine."

"Tracy, read what you and Nora can do at the Clip 'n' Curl," Jen said.

Tracy pushed back her long blonde hair and read: " 'One: You cannot cut, set, perm, color, or *touch* anyone's hair. You cannot do nails. You cannot do pedicures. Two: You cannot go near the cash register. The cashier will do that. Three: You can bring coffee and magazines to the customers. Four: You can write down appointments in the appointment book. Five: You can hang up coats.' "

"That's exciting," Nora said.

"It's better than filling ketchup containers," Jen answered.

"I think it's fine," Tracy said. "And we'll have a chance to read all those great magazines."

"Okay, Denise and Lucy, what are your instructions?" Mrs. Ryan asked.

Lucy looked at the paper she held in her hand. " 'One: You cannot in any way alter the clothes. Two: You cannot tell a customer she looks good in something that she looks awful in, just to sell it. Three: You cannot offer a garment for anything more or less than is on the price tag.' "

Denise took over. " 'Four: You cannot rearrange the stock. Five: You cannot change the window display. Six: You can sell anything as long as you obey the above instructions.' "

Andy and Mia looked at their list. " 'One: You cannot try to change the customers' minds about what they want to buy, even if you hate the record they like. Two: You cannot work the cash register. Three: You cannot use the loudspeaker to have music playing outside the store. Four: You can sell to the customers. Five: You can suggest records, if the customer is uncertain. Six: You can wrap packages.' "

"Now me," Jason said. " 'One: You cannot go near the projection booth. Two: You cannot work the popcorn machine. Three: You cannot fool around with the lights in the theater.' "

"Okay," Susan said. "Don't hog things. 'Four: You can usher people to their seats. Five: You can clean the theater between shows. Six: You can sell packaged candy at the candy counter.' "

Mitch and Tommy then read their list. " 'One: You cannot throw balls around the store. Two: You cannot demonstrate any of the equipment. Three: You cannot work the cash register. Four: You can sell to the customers. Five: You can explain how things work. Six: You can wrap packages, if you know how.' "

"Now that everyone has read," Mrs. Ryan said, "there is one other thing. The owners have all spoken with me, and they all insist that one of their adult employees be on the premises. That adult will be the one to take care of the money matters."

Jen frowned. "I thought *we* were running things. What is this adult business?"

"You will be running things, Jen," Mrs. Ryan said. "The adult will just take care of the cash register. You can't expect the owners to take the chance of you messing up all their accounting."

"Who says we would mess up?" Nora asked.

Her mother turned to her. "I think these mall people are being very cooperative. And if that is what they feel has to be, you kids have to go along with it. I have been assured the employee will not interfere in any way."

"I guess we have no choice," Steve said.

"Right," Mrs. Ryan said. "Now, tomorrow is Saturday. You are all to go to your stores and let the owners show you everything you have to know to take over. Then, they all agreed that Monday is the day. From five to eight."

"So soon?" Steve asked nervously.

Mrs. Ryan smiled. "Well, they all seemed to feel they wanted to get it over with."

"*That's* encouraging," Denise said, frowning.

"Mr. Hendrix has spoken to the newspaper. They will carry a big story about this on Sunday. So you'll have plenty of publicity," Jessica Ryan said. "I wish you all lots of luck and . . . *behave.*"

Chapter 6

The next night Nora slept over at Jen's. They were sprawled out on the twin beds in Jen's room, watching a horror movie on TV, eating the granola bars that Nora had brought, and comparing their experiences that afternoon.

"I never realized that a beauty parlor smelled so, well . . . beauty parlorish. It gets to be a bit much after a while." Nora wrinkled her small nose.

Jen giggled. "You were only there a little while. What are you going to do Monday night? Anyway, it smells better than the Burger Barn. All that *food*, constantly cooking."

There was a knock on the door and Jen called out, "Come in."

"You have to open the door," Jeff answered. "I can't."

With a puzzled look at Nora, Jen got off the bed and opened the bedroom door. Jeff stood there with a tray. He came into the room and said, "Room service, my ladies. The best hot chocolate *with* marshmallows. Real, fresh cookies, and a bowl of fruit." He put the tray on Jen's desk and smiled at the girls. "Okay, dig in."

After they had each taken a cup of the rich, dark chocolate and a cookie, they got back on the beds. Jeff stood and watched them. "All ready for the big night Monday?"

Jeff's blue eyes under thick, bushy gray eyebrows caught the sudden, worried expression on Jen's face. "What's up?"

Jen looked embarrassed. "What do I know about a hamburger place?" she asked. "I mean, I hardly know how to cook one here."

"You're not supposed to cook them. Remember?" Jeff asked.

"I guess," Jen said. "But suddenly this doesn't seem to be as good an idea as I thought. Only, you both have to promise not to breathe a word to anyone that I said that."

Nora nodded. "What do I know about a beauty parlor? I hardly ever go, and when I did, they ruined me. I know more about hamburgers. So I don't exactly feel great confidence, Jen."

Jen looked at Jeff, who was now straddling the desk chair. "What should I wear, Jeff? I want to look . . . well . . . mature."

Jeff stood up. "I tell you what . . . you two talk about what clothes to wear. That will take your minds off the rest of the things you're worried about. I have the kitchen floor to wax and Debby is coming over to watch me do it."

"What *should* we wear?" Nora asked after Jeff left the room.

"Well," Jen said, "you should look glamorous and I should look . . ."

"Like a dietician," Nora said.

"What does a dietician look like?" Jen asked, laughing.

"How should I know?" Nora said. "Okay, you're right. I have to look glamorous and you should look efficient. Wear your navy pants and that white turtleneck sweater with a bright scarf around your neck. Only, don't get ketchup on the sweater."

"Right," Jen said. "And you wear that long, flowered skirt and your light blue silk blouse."

Suddenly, Nora pointed at the screen. "The monster is eating the house!" she yelled.

The next morning there was a front page story in the Cedar Groves Herald:

EIGHTH-GRADERS TAKE OVER MONDAY NIGHT
Will the Mall Ever Be the Same?

Cedar Groves: A group of enterprising, creative eighth-graders will run some of the establishments at the Twin Rivers Mall tomorrow evening from five to eight to raise money for the new town swimming pool.

The following are the students involved and where they will be:

Denise Hendrix and *Lucy Armanson* will take over the *Chic Boutique*.

Jennifer Mann and *Steve Crowley* will be at the *Burger Barn*.

Nora Ryan and *Tracy Douglas* can be seen at *Clip 'N' Curl*.

Andy Warwick and *Mia Stevens* will be ready for you at the *Record Mart*.

Jason Anthony and *Susan Hillard* will be at the *Mall Cinema*.

Mitch Pauley and *Tommy Ryder* will be at Norton's Sporting Goods.

Give these eighth-graders all your support by going to the stores and buying something. Don't just look, BUY.

Good luck, kids.

Jen and Nora read the article breathlessly. Then Jen ran into the kitchen, waving the paper. "Look," she yelled to her father, who was sitting at the kitchen table drinking a cup of coffee. "Our names are in the paper. I'm famous."

Nora pushed in after Jen. "What about me? My name is there, too. All our names are there, Jen. We're *all* famous!"

The next day in school, the eighth-graders could hardly sit in their seats. The only class that was bearable for them was Ms. Dalton's social studies class. She had been in charge of the Great Eighth Grade Switch, where they had all gone to live in another student's home for a week. So she understood their excitement and concern.

"Okay," she said. "Anyone have anything special to say? Any questions to ask? Speak now or forever hold your peace."

"Can I take my skateboard?" Jason asked.

"What should we wear?" Tommy called out.

"How can I stand Jason?" Susan asked.

"Can I get my hair done at the Clip 'n' Curl?" Tracy wondered.

"Do we get a discount on clothes at the boutique?" Denise asked.

Ms. Dalton smiled. "There is not one important question in the lot. Anyone scared?"

Mitch hooted. "What's to be scared about?"

"I just hope you don't find out," Jen answered.

"I'm scared," Denise said. "I've never worked in my whole life."

"Live and learn," Lucy said. "But why do I have to be the one you're going to be learning with?"

Ms. Dalton held her hand up. "Enough. Okay. You all know what to do. Be in your proper places at five . . . get there a little before five so you can get settled. I'll stop by to see all of you. Good luck. You're going to do great."

After school they all raced home. They showered and dressed and changed clothes at least twice. They gazed into mirrors and snipped stray pieces of hair. They fixed snacks to eat and some of them were able to eat and others just looked at the food and turned away from it, unable to think about eating, with the way their stomachs were churning. And then it was time. They were ready.

Chapter 7

They were all in the right places at the right time. They had their final instructions from nervous owners who were obviously reluctant to leave their stores. But at last, with backward glances of concern, the owners left. And the eighth-graders were on their own.

At the Mall Cinema, Susan and Jason stood inside the dark theater and watched carefully for any patron to come in and look for a seat. Since the new show didn't begin until six o'clock, there weren't many people coming in, but one man did. Jason and Susan raced over to him with their flashlights on.

"Where would you like to sit?" Susan asked eagerly.

"In a seat," the man said. "You one of those kids running the mall?"

"Sure am," Jason said, pushing Susan aside.

Susan pushed Jason back. "Stop it. I saw him first," she said angrily.

"Keep quiet. I can't hear the movie with all that noise," someone near them said.

Susan took the man's arm and carefully ushered him to a seat.

"It's too far front," the man complained. "I need something farther back."

"Of course, you do," Jason said. "Follow me." He smiled superiorly at Susan. "I know where men like to sit."

"My wife likes to sit in the back, too," the man said. "She's in New York visiting her mother. You know you get lonesome when your wife goes away."

"SSSH! Will you people stop the noise?" a woman shouted. "I'm going to ask for my money back if this keeps up."

Susan pulled Jason to the back of the theater. "Great!" she said. "All we need is to have to give money *back*. That will help the pool. Just keep quiet, Jason."

Suddenly a loud voice echoed through the theater. "Mona. Mona, where are you?"

A distraught young woman was wandering up and down the aisles, looking in all the seats. "MONA! You answer me or you're not going to another movie for a year. Where are you?"

"SHUT UP," an angry man yelled. "Can't anyone keep order in this place?"

Jason and Susan hurried up to the woman, and Jason put a hand on her arm. "Madam, you have to be quiet," he whispered.

"Quiet?" she exclaimed. "Quiet, when my child is missing? And you, young man, take your hand off me or I'll have you arrested for assault."

"Assault," Jason yelped. "Lady, you can't mean that."

"MONA," the woman yelled again. "You come right to me or you'll be sorry."

Suddenly an arm reached out in the dark and circled Susan's leg. She shrieked and clutched Jason's arm. When he felt the arm on him, he shrieked, too.

"It's just me," a child's voice said. "Mommy, here I am."

Susan flashed her light into the child's face. "You shouldn't grab people in the dark, you monster," she said.

The young mother turned on Susan with rage. "*Who* are you calling a monster, you monster? How dare you? I want my money back for this rudeness."

By now everyone in the theater was on their

feet, stamping, yelling, calling for silence. And at that very moment, the movie disappeared from the screen.

"Now what?" someone yelled.

A voice came down from the projection booth. "Calm down. The projector seems to have broken. I'll have it fixed in a jiffy. Everyone sit down."

The woman left, dragging her child after her. "I'll take this up with the manager tomorrow. You kids don't know anything about customer relations."

The lights went on in the theater and music played, while the patrons clapped and whistled and stamped their feet.

"What are we going to do?" Susan asked Jason desperately.

Jason looked around at the angry people and said, "Don't worry. I know just the thing. All they need is a little distraction."

He disappeared and a few minutes later he appeared on the brightly lit stage of the theater with his skateboard. His red hair shone under the lights. "Ladies and gentlemen, while you are waiting for the movie, you will be fortunate to see a startling exhibition of skateboarding."

Jason began skateboarding around the stage. He bowed between each trick that he did until the booing and shouting started.

"Get off that stage. Get the movie going."

"Kid, disappear."

"I'm going. Who needs this?"

"I want my money back."

Jason kept skating around the stage until Susan appeared and pulled him off. "Are you crazy? *You* are going to cause a riot. Go find out what's happening in the projection booth."

Jason climbed up to the booth and found the projectionist busy trying to get things going again. "Okay, kid, don't panic. Tell them five more minutes."

Jason ran down the stairs and onto the stage. As soon as he appeared the booing started again. "Go away!" a patron yelled.

Jason held up his hands and bowed. "Five minutes and the movie will be on again."

And it was. It only had ten more minutes to run and then the theater began emptying. But the delay meant that the usual twenty minutes between shows would have to be cut to five. Five minutes to clean the theater and get the six o'clock patrons in and seated! Susan ran outside and her mouth dropped open as she gazed at the long line of people waiting to buy tickets and get into the theater.

She said to the cashier, "Take your time selling tickets. We aren't ready for this mob. Not at all."

The cashier looked at Susan and shook her head despairingly. "You kids. My job is to sell tickets and get the people in and that's what I'm going to do. So get the theater cleaned up and get these people seated."

Susan ran back into the theater. She and Jason rushed up and down the aisles, grabbing popcorn containers and empty soda cans. One of the other ushers laughed. "I like to see people working hard." He leaned idly against a seat as he spoke.

Jason stopped picking up the debris and stood up tall. "I'm the boss for three hours and if you want to keep your job, clean this place up."

The usher laughed again. "You're too much. Relax, Anthony. Don't play the big shot. I'll be here long after you're gone."

Jason looked at the usher and walked away. Being a boss was harder than he thought it would be.

He and Susan kept running around trying to clean up. But as they were doing it the new customers were coming in and looking for seats.

"Why is the theater so filthy?" a man asked Susan.

Susan, being her usual nasty self, looked at the man and narrowed her eyes. "If it isn't clean enough for you, why don't *you* help clean it?" She thrust a plastic bag half-filled with garbage at him.

The man just stared. "You are one fresh kid."

Jason pushed Susan out of the way and pulled a seat down for the man. "I'm sorry, sir. She's just a little upset today. Have a seat."

"Don't you talk about me," Susan said. "I'm not upset."

"Do you want me to tell him you're always this way . . . mean and tactless?" Jason asked.

"Hey, my seat is full of some sticky cola," a woman shouted. "Someone come and clean it off."

Jason leaned against an empty seat and wiped his forehead, which was damp with sweat. "Whose idea was this whole thing anyway?"

At last the theater was full, the lights went down, and the movie began. Jason sank into an empty seat in the back of the theater to watch the movie. He began to relax and enjoy himself. This wasn't so bad after all, he thought. You just had to cool it. Not get hysterical. Why, he could manage all this easily.

Suddenly he felt someone shaking him violently. Susan crouched down next to his seat and whispered, "Get out of that seat and come with me. *Now!*"

Jason got up quickly and followed Susan. In the lobby she turned to him and said angrily, "You didn't pay for a ticket, so what makes you think you can just sit and watch the movie? Anyway, there is a man over there with a big complaint. Talk to him."

Jason looked over to where Susan was pointing. An old, white-haired man was looking at them. "Why don't *you* take care of whatever the problem is. You think you're so smart," Jason said.

"Why don't I? Why don't I?" Susan shouted. "Because the girl who works at the candy counter just quit. She says she isn't working for kids . . . just because I told her she couldn't take a dinner break. So I have to take her place at the counter."

"Why did you tell her she couldn't take a break?" Jason asked.

"I thought it would be more efficient if everyone kept working . . . that's why. And it would be, too. She didn't have to have dinner just then."

"Sure, it's more efficient," Jason said sarcastically, "especially since she quit."

"Just go and talk to that old man," Susan said. "Don't give me a hard time, because *I'm* ready to quit."

Jason walked over to the man. "What seems to be the problem, sir?"

"It's that young couple in front of me in the balcony," the man said. "All they do is kiss and hug and I can't see because their heads are so close together."

"Well," Jason said, "why don't you just change your seat?"

"Young man, first of all there is no other seat to move to. Second of all, I came to see them kissing on the screen, not in the seats in front of me. Are you going to talk to them or am I going to have to get my money back?"

"Why does everyone want their money back?" Jason asked.

"Maybe because they're not satisfied," the old man said. "Ever think of that? Now come on, I want you to talk to those kids in front of me. You're the manager tonight, aren't you?"

Jason thought, He's right. *I'm* the manager.

They walked up to the balcony and the man showed Jason where he was sitting. Right in front of the seat was the couple. Her curly blonde head was right next to his dark-haired one. Every few minutes the boy would turn and kiss the girl and then they would bring their heads back together again, blocking the view from where the old man was sitting.

"Say something to them," the man ordered.

Jason cleared his throat and tapped the boy on the shoulder. "Can we talk?" Jason asked.

"Of course not," the boy whispered. "The movie is on."

"Look," Jason said. "You're going to have to go someplace else if you're just going to sit and kiss. Movies aren't the place for that."

"They're not?" the girl asked in a puzzled tone of voice.

"If we had someplace else to go, we wouldn't be *here*," the boy said.

"Go home," Jason said.

"Oh sure," the girl answered. "I have four brothers and sisters and he has five. A lot of privacy we have at home. This is just about the only place we can come and just hug and kiss."

Jason was filled with sympathy for the couple. "Did you hear that?" he asked the old man. "It's pathetic."

"And expensive, too," the girl said.

The old man looked at the couple. "I guess you can't beat young love." He turned to Jason. "Okay, just give me my money back and I'll leave."

"Sir," Jason said, "You don't understand. We are trying to raise money for the Cedar Groves Pool. If I give everyone their money back who asked for it tonight, we wouldn't have made anything. Can't you just look over their heads?"

The man sank back in his seat. "Okay. Okay. Just keep quiet so I can hear the movie, even if I can't see it."

Just then the movie ended. Everyone started getting up, dumping popcorn and soda cans on the floor. The lights went on, and Jason looked at his watch. It was twenty to eight. Twenty minutes and he'd be free. He went downstairs and into the lobby. Susan's candy counter was surrounded by people coming in who wanted food.

"Line up," she shouted. "Don't push. If you don't get waited on, it's better for your health anyway. Junk food isn't good for you. So just stop shoving."

"What kind of service is this?" a woman asked. "My kid wants some popcorn."

Everyone started yelling out what they wanted. Jason was about to go behind the counter to help Susan when the usher shouted that the eight o'clock movie was about to begin. The crowd around the counter pushed to the entrance to the theater, knocking Jason down in their rush. He sat on the floor and put his head in his hands. Suddenly Pete Tabor appeared.

"Okay kids, you can go now," he said happily, ignoring Jason's position. "It's eight o'clock. *It's over*. How did it go?"

Susan and Jason exchanged looks. "Fine, Mr. Tabor. Just fine. A piece of cake," Jason said.

Susan leaned wearily against the candy counter. "Sure. *Just fine*."

Chapter 8

Mia and Andy arrived at the Record Mart, eager and ready to work. George Paley showed them around the store once again and introduced them, again, to the twenty-year-old cashier, who nodded curtly at them.

Mia, who thought she had dressed in a more subdued way, noticed that her combination of pink pants and an orange top to match her orange hair made the cashier blink. Andy was all in black, including a black leather band around his neck and one around his wrist.

Mr. Paley, noting his cashier's look, said, "Now, Renee, I'm sure the kids will do just fine. You just help them out in any way you can."

Renee shrugged. "Who's going to help me? I have a terrible feeling I'm going to need it."

George Paley just shook his head. "It's five o'clock . . . time for me to go. Now don't forget

. . . you call if anything goes wrong."

"Nothing is going to go wrong," Mia said firmly.

"Want to bet?" Renee asked.

"Please, Renee," Mr. Paley begged. "Just be cooperative."

"I'm cooperative," Renee said. "Miss Cooperative, that's me."

"Sure," Andy whispered under his breath. Mia nudged him hard in the ribs.

The Record Mart wasn't a huge store, but it was well stocked with every kind of record. It didn't only depend on the teenagers for customers, but sold classical music, opera, and the big bands. When Mr. Paley left, there were only a few customers who were browsing. Finally, a woman came over with an album of the sound track from *The Glenn Miller Story*.

"What's *The Glenn Miller Story* and who was Glenn Miller?" Andy asked.

The woman looked surprised. "*The Glenn Miller Story* is an old movie about Glenn Miller, who had one of the best big bands in the forties."

"Wouldn't you like something a little more modern?" Andy asked, holding the album as if it might explode at any minute.

"If I wanted something more modern, I

would have picked out something more modern," the woman said, her voice rising so that it could be heard all over the store.

Mia came running over and said breathlessly, "Can I help you, madam?"

The customer looked at Mia's spiked orange hair and the pink and orange clothes she had on. "I doubt it."

Mia took the record out of the woman's hands and looked at it quickly. "An excellent choice. Miller is a great musician."

The customer breathed a sigh of relief. "I agree. Now, can you wrap the record for me and tell me how much I owe you?"

Mia walked over to the wrapping desk and put the record into a plastic bag. The cashier wrote out a sales slip and took the money. As the customer started to leave, she looked at Mia and Andy. "I guess you are part of that thing about the students running the mall tonight."

Mia smiled and nodded. The woman took Mia aside and said in a low voice, "Honey, you're okay, but I wouldn't let that boy wait on too many people."

When she had gone, Andy asked, "What did she say to you?"

"She said she thought we were both very helpful," Mia answered.

"I think you're lying," Andy said. "But I also don't want to know the truth." He started to straighten a pile of records and then he turned back to Mia. "How do you know who Glenn Miller is?"

"I don't," Mia said.

Andy raised his eyebrows. "But you said to the lady that she had made an excellent choice and that Miller was a great musician."

Mia looked at Andy proudly. "That's what is known as establishing good customer relations. I'm obviously a born salesperson."

Andy snickered. "I'm as good as you are any day. I just wasn't trying."

"Or thinking," Mia said with disdain.

Andy was about to answer her when a crowd of junior high students came into the store. Soon another group followed them. Suddenly the Record Mart was filled with kids swarming up and down the aisles. They pulled records out of their slots, stood reading the backs of the covers, and some sang the songs on the records loudly. Renee watched them and then, unable to keep track of where all the students were, put her head in her hands. The noise was deafening.

Finally Renee motioned to Mia to come over to her. "What are you going to do about this?" she asked Mia.

"Do about what? Look at all the customers we have. It's wonderful."

Renee grimaced. "Oh sure, wonderful. Mia, you don't have customers . . . you have browsers. There's a difference. I don't see anyone buying anything. *And*, there are so many kids in here now I can't keep my eyes on all of them at the same time."

Mia looked around the store. "So? Don't keep your eyes on them."

Renee shook her head in dispair. "Have you ever heard of shoplifting? Do you know how many records disappear from a store like this in one day? You're pretty naive, kid."

Mia turned away from Renee and peered at the crowd in the store. "Most of these kids are my friends. They're not shoplifters."

"As far as I'm concerned — and so is Mr. Paley, by the way — *anyone* is a potential shoplifter. Not just the kids, either. The guy that looks like anybody's favorite dad or granddad can walk out of the store with a record and 'forget' to pay for it."

Mia's shoulders slumped and she ran her hand through her spiked hair.

"Just keep your eyes open, kid. And tell your boyfriend, too. If you can wrench him away from his blocks."

Mia turned and stared at Andy. He was

trying to see how high he could build a pile of records. A crowd of his friends were around him, encouraging him with shouts of, "One more, Andy boy. One more."

Mia ran over to him and yelled, "Andy! *What* are you doing?"

Andy turned quickly to Mia and his elbow hit the pile of records. It cascaded to the floor, spreading out over a few feet.

"Now, look what you made me do," Andy said angrily. "If anything is broken, it's your fault, Mia."

"*My* fault," Mia shouted back. "You're the one who was acting like a two-year-old, not me."

Their friends gathered around them. "You tell him, Mia," a girl yelled.

"Don't let her talk to you that way," a boy shouted.

Mia put the fingers of her right hand into her mouth and blew the loudest whistle she could. The store suddenly became silent. "Now all of you listen to me. You can't just mill around here, blocking the aisles, discouraging other customers from coming in, and making a mess out of things. Either you buy something or you have to get out."

Andy pulled at Mia's arm. "You can't do that. These are my friends."

"Then *you* tell your friends to get out," Mia said.

"No way. *You* are a fink, Mia."

Mia lifted her chin. "I'm trying to run this store and make money. And that's what I'm going to do . . . make money."

She faced the crowd again. "Okay, kids, if you buy one record album, you get one 45 for half price. That's a good offer . . . take advantage of it."

Renee ran over to Mia and pulled at her arm, as Andy had. "What's with you? Who said you could give the store away? Are you nuts, or something?"

Mia shook Renee's hand loose. "Will everyone stop pulling at me? And I'm not giving the store away. Just look at what is going on!"

Renee and Mia looked around the store. The junior high crowd were all seriously looking through the records . . . all obviously ready to buy one. Some of them were already lined up at the cashier's desk, waiting to pay.

Renee smiled for a moment and then went back to her usual frown. "I don't know . . . Mr. Paley might not like this." But she went to the cash register and started taking the money.

Andy looked at the line, too. "Hey, we're doing pretty good."

"*We're* doing good?" Mia said. "All you've

done is try to build a tower of records. And you didn't even succeed at that."

"You think you're so smart," Andy said. "So you're giving half the stock away to our friends. But just look around — there isn't one adult in the store. You can't run a store on just what kids buy." Andy looked at Mia with satisfaction. "You think you're the only one who knows anything about customer relations."

"Okay," Mia said, "so think of some way to get the adults to come in."

"Who, me?" Andy asked with surprise.

"Who else," Mia asked, looking at a gray-haired man going through the Frank Sinatra records.

Andy frowned and pulled at the black leather collar around his neck. "I'll think of something. Don't you worry."

Mia walked over to the man looking at the Sinatra records. "May I help you?"

"I'll take these two," the man said, handing Mia the records. He looked around the store. "I haven't been in here for a while. It seems as if the kids are always filling up the place. And their music . . . well, it just isn't my kind, you know." He smiled and poked at the Sinatra records. "Now this guy . . . he's from my time."

"Who else is from your time?" Mia asked.

The man looked nostalgic, as if he were far

back in another period. "Miller; the Dorsey boys, Tommy and Jimmy; Benny Goodman; Artie Shaw. Those were the people playing when I was a teenager. They were good, too. Don't you think they weren't."

Mia gave the man his package and looked thoughtful as she watched him leave the store. She walked over to Renee and said, "How do you start the loudspeaker that plays music outside the store?"

"Oh, no," Renee said immediately. "That's one of the things you aren't supposed to fool around with. Mr. Paley told me very definitely . . . you aren't allowed to use the loudspeaker."

Mia motioned to Andy to come over to her. "Find me a Benny Goodman album," she said.

"Who?" Andy asked.

"Benny Goodman," Mia repeated. "He was probably a bandleader. Just find a record."

Andy went off muttering to himself. "Never heard of him."

Mia turned her attention back to Renee. "Look, I have an idea that I think will bring some grown-ups in the store. If it works, and we sell a lot of records, I'll tell Mr. Paley you helped me."

"And if it doesn't work?" Renee asked.

"I'll tell Mr. Paley you didn't have anything to do with it."

"That's fair," Renee said. "You stay here and watch the store and I'll set the machine up."

After five minutes she came back. "It's ready. Just put any record you want on the turntable and you're in business."

Mia got the Goodman record from Andy and soon music was coming out of the loudspeaker and drifting through the mall. As if they were following the Pied Piper, people began moving toward where the music was coming from. They were almost all older people, although some younger people who liked swing music stopped to listen, too. But it was the older ones who came into the store and started going through the records. Soon many of them were lined up waiting to pay for their purchases. Renee nodded her head at Mia and smiled.

"It's been a long time since we've heard this kind of music coming out of this store," a woman waiting on line said. "It sounds great. And since I want to help you kids raise money for the pool, I'm going to buy three records."

Someone else on line called out to friends browsing through the records, "Buy some. Let's give these kids a hand."

Mia kept the music going all evening, and the store was filled with both young and old people . . . all buying. Renee could hardly keep up with the business.

But then, Mia, who had watched everyone carefully, gasped as she saw a young man stealthily take a record, put it in his attaché case, and start out of the store. She began to move after him. Renee put a hand on her arm.

"You can't do that. He has to go out of the store with the merchandise before you can stop him. Otherwise he can say he intended to pay for the record, and you're in trouble. It's like libel or something."

Mia watched the man and as soon as he left the store she took off after him. "Mia, be careful," Renee shouted.

Outside Mia put her hand on the man's arm and smiled innocently at him. "Sir, I *know* you didn't mean to do this. I *know* it was a mistake, but you put a record in your case there and you forgot to pay for it before you left the store."

Mia's eyes moved to a police officer leaning against a phone booth. The young man's eyes followed Mia's. He cleared his throat. "Well, now, how about that? You're right, I just forgot. How could I have done that?"

Mia smiled even more broadly, thinking to herself, What a liar you are. Aloud she said, "Well, why don't you just come inside and pay Renee for the record? Then everything will be just fine."

Renee's eyes widened with surprise as the man and Mia walked to her cash register. "You're really too much," she whispered to Mia. "That took guts . . . lots of guts."

Mia smiled and was about to tell Andy what had happened when she realized he would just think she was bragging. She had a terrible feeling her boyfriend was not impressed with her performance in the store. At the moment, Andy was staring blankly at a woman, who was gesturing impatiently. Mia walked over in time to hear the woman saying, "I want to help you raise money for the pool, but honestly, you're making it very hard."

Once again Mia smiled and said, "Can I help?"

Andy said, "She wants some guy named Shosto something or other. I think she's making the name up. No one could have a name like that."

"I want Shostakovich's Ninth Symphony. Dimitri Shostakovich. He was a Russian — "

"I know who he was," Mia interrupted. "My mother has some of his records. I'll get the symphony for you."

Andy glared at Mia's back. "She thinks she knows everything."

The woman looked at Andy. "And just because she knows something you don't know

. . . that upsets you. Right? Men!"

Mr. Paley appeared at Andy's elbow. "It's ten to eight, almost time for you kids to leave. And you tell me why the loudspeaker is going when I told you you couldn't touch it?"

"Don't ask me," Andy said. "It was Mia's idea. Not mine. She's run this whole show. She wouldn't listen to me about anything."

Mr. Paley narrowed his lips. "Where is that girl? I want to talk to her!"

Mia returned then with the record in her hand. She handed it to the customer. "Here it is . . . Shostakovich's Ninth. Enjoy it."

Mr. Paley waited until the woman had gone before he turned to Mia and said angrily, "I thought I told you not to touch the loud-speaker."

"I know Mr. Paley, but . . ." Tears began to come into Mia's eyes. She was tired. Andy hated her. And now Mr. Paley was yelling at her.

"Not buts. You didn't live up to the rules."

Renee came over and shook her finger at Mr. Paley. "Before you yell at this kid, look around the store. You haven't had this many people in here in months. And half of them are in here because *she* put Benny Goodman on the loudspeaker."

George Paley looked around him and then at

the people lined up to buy records. He turned back to Mia. "Well, what are you waiting for? Go back to work." His voice was harsh, but he was smiling.

Mia grinned and started over to a customer. Mr. Paley stopped her. "I could use someone on Saturdays. Interested?"

"You bet," Mia said. "Come on, Andy, let's get back to work."

Andy shook his head. "It's eight o'clock. I've had it. Anyway, he wants you . . . not me." He gave Mia an angry look and walked out of the store.

Mia watched him go, not knowing what to do. She could run after him and make up . . . right now . . . or she could stay and work. She looked over at Renee.

"I can't help you with this one, kid. You have to decide what to do all by yourself."

Mia bit her lip and tried to think clearly. The store was filled. People were waiting to be helped . . . to ask questions. Mia stood up tall and walked over to a customer. She had done a good job that night. And she wasn't going to leave it.

"May I help you?" Mia asked.

Chapter 9

The Chic Boutique had only one customer when
Denise and Lucy arrived. Ms. Garston was
helping a young woman who was trying to decide between two skirts . . . one long and one
short. Denise walked over to the owner and
said, "We'll take care of everything, Ms. Garston. You can go now."

The customer looked up in surprise. "Go?"
Then she smiled. "Oh, sure, you're the kids who
are running the mall. Okay, help me decide
which of these skirts to buy."

"The long one," Lucy said.

"The short one," Denise said.

"Great!" Ms. Garston said. "I'm going before
I change my mind about this whole thing. I'll
be back at eight . . . on the dot."

"Why did you say the long one?" Denise

asked Lucy. "Short is the rage now. And this customer has such good legs."

The customer smiled, obviously pleased with Denise's comment. "Thanks."

Lucy, not to be outdone, said, "Of course she has good legs, but short is just as you said, 'the rage'; in a little while it will be out of style. Long is going to be chic forever."

Ignoring the customer, who now looked puzzled, Denise said, "Well, don't people want to be in style now? You don't want to go around looking like last year's fashion magazine."

"And what about when the rage isn't the rage anymore?" Lucy asked.

Denise shrugged, "So you buy something else."

Lucy looked very self-satisfied. "Exactly! That's your point of view because you're rich. But everyone doesn't have the money to buy new clothes every year . . . so they need things that will be fashionable for a long time. Long is safer."

The customer looked at Lucy and nodded her head in agreement. "The young lady is right. I sure don't have the money to buy new clothes every time some person in Paris decides to get women to spend more money. I'll take the long one."

Lucy took the skirt and wrapped it carefully.

Meanwhile, the customer handed Denise a credit card. Denise looked at it and then walked over to Lucy. She whispered, "I don't know how to do whatever you do with this."

Lucy grinned. "You sure know how to use it to buy stuff with. It's okay, I know what to do."

"How come?" Denise asked.

"I worked at the kiddie shop on Saturdays once. I learned the routine with credit cards there. Give the lady the package and I'll charge the skirt."

As soon as the customer left, two men came into the shop. The girls hurried over to them. "Can I help you?" Denise asked.

"Well, I'm looking for a birthday present for my wife. Maybe a blouse." The man turned to his friend. "Think that's a good idea, Ben?"

Ben shrugged. "I guess that's okay. You know what she'd like, Dave. She's *your* wife."

Dave didn't look too sure that he knew what she'd like. He walked around the shop aimlessly and finally sank down into a small green velvet chair. "Sure. A blouse is fine. Perfect in fact."

Lucy asked with a smile, "What style? Tailored or dressy?"

The man thought for a minute. "Dressy, I guess. Yeah, like to go out to dinner in. I'm taking her out for her birthday to that new, fancy place in town."

"What color?" Denise asked patiently.

"Color?" the man repeated. "What color, Ben?" he asked his friend.

Ben looked as puzzled as Dave did. "Listen, I have enough trouble buying my own wife presents. You're on your own in this."

Dave looked at the shirt Denise had on. "That's pretty. What color would you call that?"

Lucy could hardly keep herself from laughing out loud. "It's turquoise. Is that the color you want?"

"Why not," Dave said. "Sure, that's great."

"Fine," Lucy said. "We're making real progress here. Now what size?"

"Oh, no." Dave moaned. "I don't know." He looked at Lucy carefully. "She's about your size, I think . . . maybe a little bigger . . . but not much."

Lucy nodded. "Okay, I'm a size six, so I'll give you an eight for your wife."

The man sighed with relief. "Fine. Eight sounds just right. Doesn't that sound right to you, Ben?"

Ben narrowed his eyes and thought. "I think she's bigger than an eight. What comes after eight?" he asked Lucy.

Lucy turned away so that the men couldn't see her laughing. Denise said quickly, "Ten. Ten comes next."

"Ten is too big. I know it," Dave said. "Eight is fine."

Lucy and Denise went to the rack of blouses and picked out a softly draped silk blouse in the right color and the right size. Denise whispered to Lucy, "Do you think *all* our customers are going to be like that? If so, I'm going to scream."

"Don't do anything to scare away the customers," Lucy said. "If you have to scream, go outside and do it."

"Some friend you are," Denise mumbled.

They brought the blouse out to the men. Dave looked at it with admiration. "Say, that's just right. You kids are smart. You can wait on me any day. I'll take it."

"You didn't ask how much it is," Lucy said.

Denise poked her in the arm and glared at her.

"Oh, yeah. How much?"

Lucy told Dave and he smiled. "It's fine. Like I said, I'll take it."

When the men left, Denise said to Lucy, "Why did you say that? You could have ruined the sale."

Lucy just laughed and playfully pushed Denise away from her. "Denise, you're so used to being rich that you don't realize everyone in this world doesn't have a lot of money . . . and they like salespeople to respect that. I know I do."

Denise went over to a mirror and adjusted the hairband that held her long blonde hair away from her face. "I know, you're right. I do forget that." She walked over to a rack and held up a pale pink T-shirt with silver sequins embroidered on it. "Hey, Lucy, you'd look great in this. Try it on."

"How much is it, Denise?" Lucy said in a teasing voice.

Denise looked at the price tag and said in a low voice, "Forget it."

Suddenly the store was filled with their friends, looking at everything, pulling things off the racks, holding things up to them.

"This is the best job of all," one girl said.

"Do you get a discount?" someone else asked.

"What does Denise need a discount for?" someone else called out.

Lucy suddenly clapped her hands loudly. "Okay, kids! You can look, but don't touch, and don't scare the customers away . . . and no trying on, unless you're really going to buy. And don't think I won't know who is and who isn't!"

"She's becoming a tyrant," Carla Owens said. Carla, next to Susan Hillard, was the nastiest girl in the eighth grade. She was feeling particularly nasty that night because she hadn't been given a shop to run.

"She isn't a tyrant, Carla. She's just doing her job . . . and doing it perfectly, too," Denise said.

Carla stuck her tongue out at Denise and then turned a corner of the store to look at the rack of jeans. When she came back to the center of the shop, Denise asked, "See anything you like, Carla?"

"Not in here," Carla answered in a superior tone. "This is really not my kind of store. Too boring."

Carla left the shop and soon all the other girls straggled out, too, going on to the other stores the eighth-graders were running.

Denise walked back to make sure Carla hadn't messed up the rack of jeans and she suddenly yelled, "Oh, no!"

Lucy ran back to Denise. "What's wrong?"

Denise was sitting on the floor about to burst into tears. "Look what that rotten girl did."

She held up a handful of price tickets. "She pulled the tickets off about ten pairs of jeans."

Lucy sank down next to Denise and took the tickets. "What a rat she is. How can anyone be that mean? She shouldn't be allowed in the pool ever."

"If we ever *get* a pool," Denise said.

"Of course we're going to get a pool." Lucy looked at the price tickets. "But our problem now is to figure out what goes on what."

"I have a better idea," Denise said. "Let's just not let anyone buy the jeans without tickets. We'll say that they are being held for someone."

Lucy looked at Denise and shook her head in disgust. "Who is going to believe that someone is holding ten pair of jeans in different sizes?"

"We can dream, can't we?" Denise asked.

"Look," Lucy said, "we know the price of things. We can figure out what ticket goes on which jeans . . . maybe."

"How?" Denise asked wearily.

"Well, we have one thing going for us . . . we have to match the size on the tickets with the size in the jeans. Right?"

"I guess so," Denise said. "I'm getting tired, Lucy. You know, it's much harder to sell clothes than to buy them."

"Tell me about it," Lucy said, as she carefully matched the price tickets with the jeans. Soon she had them all pinned back on the pants except two. One was a ticket for $30 and one for $40.

"Which do you think belongs on which?" Lucy asked Denise.

Denise took the jeans, one pair at a time, turning them inside out to look at the seams and examine the button holes. "Okay," she said, "I'd guess that the more expensive ones are the darker jeans."

"I think you're right," Lucy said. "But what if you aren't?"

"Then some lucky girl gets a pair of jeans for ten dollars less than she should have paid," Denise said.

"Yeah," Lucy added, "and some *un*lucky girl is paying ten dollars more than she should."

"I never thought of that," Denise said. "Tell you what, if anyone complains, I'll pay her back the ten dollars."

"It's a deal," Lucy said. "And don't forget you offered."

The next hour was a busy one. Customers came and went and Lucy's eyes became brighter, her smile wider, and her feet moved faster. She was happy and excited, and the customers loved her. Denise worked hard, too, but she was getting more tired and less interested in selling the clothes as the time passed.

Whenever she could, she sat down in one of the small velvet chairs that were scattered around the store. When the store emptied for a few minutes, she took off her shoes and rubbed her feet.

"I never knew feet could feel this bad," she said to Lucy.

"I told you not to wear new shoes tonight," Lucy said.

"I wanted to look good," Denise answered.

"Yeah, but to me you'd look better on your feet, waiting on people, than sitting in those silly little chairs."

"Denise," a voice called out. "Why are you sitting down?" Barbara Hendrix, Denise's mother, was standing over her daughter.

"What are you doing here?" Denise asked her mother. "And I'm sitting down because my feet hurt."

"Not used to working hard, are you? This is good for you."

Denise frowned. "Why do you always think that anything that makes me uncomfortable is good for me? And you didn't answer me. What you are doing here?"

Mrs. Hendrix started going through a rack of silk pants. "I thought I'd buy something and help the cause." She held up a pair of yellow pants and turned to Lucy. "Like these?"

"They're gorgeous," Lucy said. "Why don't you go in a dressing room and try them on?"

Barbara Hendrix went into one of the little rooms whose walls were mirrored and whose floors were carpeted with soft blue carpet. After a while, Lucy said, "Your mother has been in there a long time. What do you suppose she's doing?"

Denise shrugged. "She always takes a long time when she tries on clothes. She looks at whatever she has on from every angle known to humankind."

"I don't know," Lucy said, as she walked back to the dressing room. "Are you okay, Mrs. Hendrix?" she called out.

"No," came a muffled answer. "I'm not okay. I seem to be locked in here."

"Just turn the knob, Mrs. Hendrix," Lucy shouted.

Denise appeared next to Lucy. "Why are you yelling?"

Lucy tried not to laugh. "Your mother said she's locked in the room."

"Don't be ridiculous," Denise said irritably. "Mother, just turn the knob."

"Denise, don't be a jerk. Don't you think if I could I would? The knob fell off. So there is nothing *to* turn. I'm locked in and I want you to get me out of here!"

Denise looked at Lucy with annoyance. "Would you believe it? My mother comes in here to help the cause, and now she's locked in. I've never been so embarrassed in my life. My mother, a grown-up, locking herself in the dressing room, like a three-year-old."

"I heard every word you said, Denise," her mother called out. "Lucy, please, *you* do something!"

"Don't worry, Mrs. Hendrix. I'll get you out. In just a few minutes."

"What are you going to do?" Denise whispered to Lucy.

"I don't know," Lucy whispered back. "You think of something. She's *your* mother."

"I'm not good at this. I've never had a mother who locked herself in a room before."

"Well, neither have I," Lucy said. "I guess there is only one thing to do."

"What's that?" Denise asked.

"Call the fire department," Lucy said. "They're good at things like this."

"Never!" Denise shouted. "I will *never* have the fire department come to get my mother out of a dressing room. I'd never live it down."

"What's going on out there?" Mrs. Hendrix called out. "Is anyone doing anything?"

"Don't worry, Mrs. Hendrix. I'm going to take care of this," Lucy replied.

"I'll tie you to a chair," Denise hissed at Lucy, "before I let you call a fireman."

"Person," Lucy said.

"Person *what*?" Denise asked.

"Fire*person*," Lucy said with annoyance. "Fireperson . . . not fireman. There are fire-women, too, you know."

"I don't believe this. My mother is locked in a dressing room. You are threatening to ruin me socially in Cedar Groves forever by calling the fire department and, on top of everything, I'm getting lectured about sexism."

"I'm not lecturing," Lucy shouted. "I'm merely correcting you."

"I'm getting angry at you two!" Mrs. Hendrix shouted. "What are you doing? I'm tired of being in here . . . and bored. And I don't like the yellow pants, either."

Denise snorted. "Mother, you come in. You lock yourself in the room and now . . . now you're not even going to buy anything."

"Denise, I'll buy something. Just get me out of here," her mother said.

"Mrs. Hendrix, I'm going to call the fire department. They'll know what to do," Lucy said.

"Good idea, Lucy. I knew I could count on you. Not like *some* people I know."

"Don't do this to me, Lucy," Denise begged.

"Have you any other ideas?" Lucy asked Denise.

Silence was her answer.

Lucy called the fire department and explained the problem. She knew she heard laughter at the other end of the line, but the man also said someone would be right over. Within ten minutes two firepersons came in to the shop . . . one was a woman.

Carefully, they took the door to the dressing room off its hinges and Mrs. Hendrix came out. "I can't thank you enough," she said to the firepersons. "I'll buy an extra book of tickets to the Fireman's Ball."

"Fire*person's* Ball," Lucy said.

"LUCY!" Denise shouted. "Not now."

Barbara Hendrix looked at her watch before she left the store and said, "Well, you only have a half an hour until Ms. Garston comes back. You should both survive. Or I should say, Denise, you'll survive. Lucy's doing more than just surviving. She's flourishing."

There was only one more customer before eight o'clock. A girl in the eighth grade came in to buy a scarf to wear with a khaki jacket. Pam Thomas wasn't known for her ability to make decisions, and Denise groaned inwardly when Pam walked into the store. She looked at at least twenty different scarfs, holding each one up to her, tying it around her neck, looking at it under a lamp. Denise kept running back to the display case to bring new ones that she though Pam might like. Finally, Pam said, "Okay, I'll take this one. How much is it?"

Denise looked at the price tag and said, "Fifteen dollars."

"Oh, no," Pam said. "I only have ten. You'll have to show me some others."

Denise rolled her eyes at Lucy and then said to Pam, "Look, take the scarf you like. I'll lend you the five dollars."

Pam looked her usual indecisive self. "I don't know when I'll be able to pay you back."

"It's all right," Denise said quickly. "Just take the scarf." And go, she added to herself. "Lucy, wrap the scarf for Pam. I'll make out the sales slip."

When Pam left, Lucy broke into laughter. "Take my advice: Never, never work as a salesperson. You'll go broke."

Denise had to laugh, too. "I never will. But you were great, Lucy. You were made to deal with people, help them make up their minds, that kind of thing. I love clothes, but I don't have the patience for this."

Lucy looked thoughtful. "You know, my father really would like me to be a doctor, like he is. He doesn't push, but I know it would make him very happy. But these three hours here have taught me something . . . I'd like to work in a place like this someday . . . and then, eventually have my own shop. I'm not meant to be a doctor."

Denise sank into a chair, took off her shoes, and starting rubbing her feet again. "Someday maybe we could go into business together. I'll do the buying of the clothes and do the display cases and windows and stuff, and you could manage the whole place and be in charge of the staff and be involved with the customers. We'd be perfect together."

Lucy smiled dreamily. "Sounds good."

Just then Ms. Garston came in. She looked around the store nervously, and when she saw that it seemed to be in one piece, she gave a sigh of relief. "How did it go?"

"Perfect," Lucy said. "No problems and we sold a lot of things, too."

"So perfect," Denise said, "that someday you are going to have competition from us. When we open our own shop, that is."

Ms. Garston smiled. "I'll be ready for you."

As the girls left the store with their arms around each other, Denise asked, "What should we call our shop?"

Chapter 10

When Steve and Jen got to the Burger Barn, it was already crowded. They went to the rest-rooms and put on their red-and-white uniforms. Jen admired herself in the mirror, especially the little red hat that sat on the back of her head. When they went back upstairs, Mr. Yancy looked around the fast-food place with a sigh of resignation and left.

Jen and Steve smiled at each other, and Steve said happily, "We're on our own."

Jen looked toward the door and saw a family with three children coming in. She hurried over to them and smiled. "Can I seat you?" she asked.

They looked startled but let her lead them to a large table. For the next fifteen minutes every person who came in the door of the Burger Barn was greeted by Jen and ushered to a table. Finally Steve came over to her and asked, "What do you think you're doing?"

"What do you mean, what am I doing? I'm being a proper hostess and taking the people to their tables."

"You don't do that in a place like this," Steve said. "This isn't a real restaurant like my dad's. It's just a Burger Barn."

"So?" Jen said. "Should I ignore people, just because it's a Burger Barn? I'm trying to add a fancy touch to the place."

Steve laughed, but Jen didn't like the tone of the laugh. "People think you're strange," Steve said. "They stare at you when you start ushering them to tables."

"And, of course, you think I'm strange, too," Jen said angrily.

"Well, you have to admit it's a little weird," Steve said, trying unsuccessfully to hide a grin.

Jen looked straight into his eyes. "You do what you want and I'll do what I want. Anyway, I don't see anyone leaving just because they are being treated well." She walked away from Steve with her head high and went up to a couple coming in the door.

After she seated the amazed couple, she looked over at Steve. One of the employees who filled orders was talking excitedly to him. The man was waving his hands around and looking back at the counter. Jen walked over to them and felt her heart sink as the employee said, "You've got to do something. We can't function at rush time when we're one short."

"Why are you one short?" Jen asked.

"Fred didn't feel well and he went home," the young man answered. "So we're one short. The orders are going to pile up back there. One of you has to help us."

Steve pushed his dark brown hair off his forehead and said confidently, "No problem. Just show me what to do."

Jen put her hand on Steve's arm. "Steve, Mr. Yancy said we aren't supposed to cook anything. Remember?"

"I'm not going to cook anything," Steve said quickly. "Just help fill the orders."

"We're not supposed to go near any of the equipment, either," Jen reminded him.

Steve looked at her with impatience. "Jen, go back to being a maitre d'. I'll take care of the orders."

Jen couldn't believe the arrogance in Steve's voice. "You have certainly changed since we walked in here. I don't think I even know you. You're a real macho type, ordering me around as if I were your lackey."

"You forget, Jen, I'm used to being around a restaurant."

"We'll see," Jen said.

Steve went behind the counter, and Jen watched everyone talking to him at once and pointing to the burgers and fries and drinks. Steve listened but Jen could see a nervous look cross his face. She giggled to herself.

Soon Steve was frantically piling things on trays. Someone yelled at him, "I said two fries and one hamburger. . . not two burgers and one fry."

Steve pulled one hamburger off the tray and reached for a bag of fries. As he put them on the tray the bag fell, spilling French fries on the floor. Steve bent to pick them up and the boy yelled, "Not now! Keep filling the orders!"

Jen sat down on a chair and watched as Steve kept whirling around trying to keep up with the instructions being shouted at him. His hat had fallen off and his shirt was pulled out of his pants. A Coke slipped from his fingers and mingled with the fries on the floor. Someone yelled, "Get a mop and wipe this muck up."

Steve looked around him for where a mop might be. A girl pointed to a supply closet in a corner and Steve started over to it . . . but he slipped on the potatoes and Coke and landed right in the mess. Jen couldn't help it — she burst out laughing, as did the rest of the help behind the counter. Steve looked over at Jen and shouted furiously, "I thought you were my friend. Why don't you get the mop? You work here, too, you know."

Jen walked over to the counter and said with wide-eyed innocence, "You're the one who is so used to being in a restaurant. I wouldn't think of interfering."

Then she felt a tap on her shoulder. A woman said with annoyance, "Do you work here?"

Jen smiled at her as charmingly as she could. "Yes, I do. How can I help you?"

"You can help me by putting towels in the women's room and by cleaning it up. It needs it . . . badly."

Jen took a breath and was about to say she didn't think that was part of her job, when Steve spoke as innocently as Jen had. "You don't think *I'm* going to the women's restroom?" he said. "And no one here can be spared. I guess you'll just have to do it, Jen."

Jen looked at him and said between clenched teeth, "I think I hate you, Steve."

She went downstairs and cleaned up the room. When she came back up she saw a small child take a ketchup container and carefully squirt the ketchup on the floor. Where is the nasty kid's mother? Jen thought. Jen ran over to the child and reached out to grab the little girl's arm. As she reached, the child started to back away and slipped, falling so that her head was in the ketchup. At that moment, the mother looked over and saw the child. She screamed a scream that reverberated throughout the Burger Barn.

"My baby," she yelled. "My baby has fallen and is bleeding! I'm going to sue this place for something!"

She ran over to her child and Jen tried to stop her to calm her down and reassure her. But the mother pushed Jen away. "Don't touch me! It's your fault! I know it."

Someone shouted, "Get a doctor!"

"No!" Jen yelled. "Don't!"

"What are you going to do?" a man asked Jen. "Let the kid bleed to death?"

"She isn't going to bleed to death," Jen said.

"How do you know?" the man asked. "Are you a doctor or something?" The man bent over to look at the child more closely. He paled.

At that moment, the child sat up, ketchup covering one side of her head. "Don't move," the mother said. "Just stay quiet, angel."

As the child sat up, the man who had been bending over her said, "I think I'm going to . . ." and then he fainted.

Steve came running over as people throughout the Burger Barn began crying out. "What's going on?" Steve asked Jen. "You've let every-thing get out of control."

Jen pushed Steve aside, as she said, "Get a glass of water for this man. He's fainted."

Steve ran for water, but the man was already coming to. Oh, get up, Jen thought, with anger. Who ever heard of fainting over a little ketchup?

Jen turned to the mother who was crying and clutching the puzzled child to her. Jen screamed over the general hysteria in the Burger Barn. "Your little girl squirted ketchup on the floor and slipped in it. It's ketchup, not blood. The kid is fine. Just clean her off . . . and don't get it all over the women's room!"

The mother looked at the child, stuck a finger into the ketchup on her head, and licked her finger. Satisfied that it *was* ketchup, she took the child's hand and turned to Jen. "How could you let that happen? You certainly aren't run-ning this place very well. I'll have to talk to Mr. Yancy about this." Then she went down to the women's room.

Steve came running back with the glass of water and held it out to the man who was now sitting up. "Where is the child?" the man asked. "The poor little thing may be dying."

"Anyone who ever died of ketchup on her

head would go down in the *Guinness Book of World Records*," Jen said.

"Ketchup?" the man repeated angrily. "What kind of trick is that to play on people? You kids!" He got up and walked out of the Burger Barn.

"He's right," Steve said. "What kind of trick is that to play on people?"

Jen glared at Steve. "You know what? I don't think I ever want to talk to you again."

"That's fine with *me*," Steve said. "You just aren't very competent."

Their angry conversation was interrupted by a frantic employee who rushed over to them. "We ran out of buns. Would you believe it, we ran out of buns?"

"That's impossible," Jen said. "Mr. Yancy would never let that happen."

"It wasn't his fault. The delivery guy never showed up today, and I guess Yancy thought we'd get through the night. But I was just in the storeroom and there are no buns. Not one."

"Don't worry," Steve said. "I'll just run over to a supermarket and buy some. What's the big deal?"

Jen laughed and turned to the employee. "How many buns do you think we will need?"

The man thought for a minute. "Well, we

close at nine, so I guess a few hundred would do it."

Jen turned to Steve. "Just make sure you have a *large* cart, Steve. Not to mention an army to carry them back here."

Steve glared at Jen. "Do you have any better ideas?"

"No," Jen said sweetly. "But then I'm just a poor little girl without any restaurant experience. Now you, you know everything."

The employee wiped his sweating forehead on his sleeve and said, "If I were you, I'd call Yancy."

"Never," Jen and Steve said together.

"Then you just have to serve the burgers without buns," the man said.

"Will anyone buy them like that?" Steve asked.

The man shrugged. "Try it and see."

Steve stood on a chair and yelled for quiet. Nobody paid any attention to him. Jen walked over to a little girl who had a whistle around her neck. "Mind if I borrow this?" she asked.

She blew the whistle three times, as hard as she could, and suddenly the place was silent. "Okay," she said to Steve. "Say whatever you want to say."

Steve cleared his throat. "We seem to have

run out of buns. So you're going to have to eat your burgers without buns."

Cries rang out. "What?"

"Not me."

"Then you have to charge less."

"I'm leaving."

"Kids!"

About half the people left, but a lot stayed and ate the burgers bunless. But by the time eight o'clock came, the Burger Barn was almost empty. When Mr. Yancy came back, he was astounded and upset. "What happened?"

Jen explained quickly.

Mr. Yancy sank into a chair. "I'm sorry, kids, really. I thought we'd get through the night. You did fine, considering."

Jen and Steve changed their clothes and left together . . . in silence. Steve looked at her out of the corner of his eye. "I'll walk you home from the bus stop," he said.

"No, thank you," Jen replied. "I may not be competent, but I do know how to walk." She ran in the direction of the bus stop, leaving Steve calling after her.

"Jen. Wait. *Please*."

Chapter 11

Tracy and Nora arrived at the Clip 'N' Curl and were met by a very nervous Tina Jacobs. "Now, remember," she said. "You aren't to touch a customer. Except to put a cape around her before the beautician starts to work."

"We remember, Ms. Jacobs," Tracy said dutifully. "We know all the rules. Don't worry."

"How can I not worry? I'm leaving my shop in the hands of babies."

"You just run along," Tracy said. "Everything is going to be fine."

Nora started at Tracy. She actually sounded confident — as if she wasn't worried about a thing!

"Come on," Tracy said. "Let's get into the uniforms."

"Uniforms?" Nora asked.

"Of course. Don't you want to look like a real

beautician? Like you really belong here?"

"I hadn't thought about it," Nora answered, but she followed Tracy into the employee dressing room. As they got in the room, Nora placed a container on a table.

"What's that?" Tracy asked.

"It's nothing," Nora said evasively.

Tracy persisted. "What do you mean, 'nothing'? It has to have something in it or you wouldn't be carting it around."

"It's just something I made . . . for the customers," Nora replied.

"*Nora!* What did you make? And what do you mean, 'for the customers'? Ms. Jacobs said. . . ."

"It's perfectly harmless," Nora interrupted. "It's just a conditioning mousse made only of natural ingredients."

"Like what kind of ingredients?" Tracy asked.

"Come on, Tracy. Get off my back. It's just egg whites and stuff. I brought along my beater. I'll just beat everything up before I use it."

"Nora, Ms. Jacobs said — "

"I know. I know," Nora said. "Let's get going."

Outside, the reception room was decorated in black and white, but the private rooms where a woman could have her hair done were all in pink. Then, for the women who were more sociable, there was a large room with eight chairs.

They went into the reception area and Tracy smiled at the woman behind the desk. Without a thought, Tracy walked over to her, held out her hand, and said, "Hi, I'm Tracy Douglas. How can I help you?"

The woman looked wary, but she held out her hand, too. "I'm Margo. You can get some coffee for the ladies in the room to the right."

Nora started at Tracy's back as her friend walked away. She really has nerve, Nora thought. Not to be outdone, Nora held out her hand, too. "Hi, I'm Nora Ryan, and you know it doesn't seem to me as if you're getting enough air circulation in this place. You know it's important for health to have a constant flow of fresh air in a place like this. Otherwise, everyone is breathing in germs and hair spray and stuff."

Margo looked at Nora and narrowed her eyes. "Are you one of these health nuts?"

Nora blushed. "What's wrong with being healthy?"

"Nothing," Margo replied, "nothing at all. Just don't upset our customers."

"What would you like *me* to do?" Nora asked.

Margo thought for a minute. "Why don't you just go straighten up the magazines."

She just wants to get rid of me, Nora fumed inwardly. Well, wait until I get a chance to use my mousse.

In the room that Margo had sent her to, Tracy was carefully bringing coffee to the customers, asking each one, "Milk? Sugar?"

One woman patted Tracy's hand as she took the coffee cup. "I'm Ms. Nesbitt. What a nice girl you are. Are you new here?"

"We're just here for tonight," Tracy answered. "To raise money for the pool, you know."

Nora came in then and walked around, asking if anyone wanted a magazine. As she asked, she fanned herself with one. "Doesn't anyone think it smells in here?"

Tracy ran over to Nora and grabbed her arm. "Don't start, Nora. Don't make trouble."

"Smells like what?" Ms. Nesbitt asked, wrinkling up her nose.

"Like perfume and spray and other unhealthy things," Nora answered.

Tracy closed her eyes for a moment, hoping when she opened them Nora would be gone. But she wasn't. Nora was bending over Ms. Nesbitt, who was waiting for her hairdresser to come. Nora picked up a strand of Ms. Nesbitt's hair and shook her head. "Your hair really needs a good conditioner."

"I just had a conditioner put on it," Ms. Nesbitt answered, looking at the hair Nora was holding up.

"Oh, sure," Nora replied knowingly. "You had one of those commercial things put on it. What you need is an all-natural conditioning mousse that will restore all the natural beauty of your hair."

Ms. Nesbitt looked up at Nora. "I didn't know they had that kind of thing here."

Nora smiled. "You just wait here and I'll bring you just what you need!" Then she ran out of the room.

Tracy ran after her, reaching for Nora's arm. "Nora, you aren't going to put one of your concoctions on Ms. Nesbitt, are you?"

"Don't sound so frightened, Tracy. It's nothing harmful and it will make her hair absolutely gorgeous."

Tracy watched as Nora opened her tote bag and took out a bowl, mixer, and a few bottles of liquids. Then she took the container of egg whites, put everything into a plastic bowl, plugged in the hand beater, and beat everything together. When she stopped, she had a bowlful of a strange-looking mixture. It smelled very strong.

Nora peered into the bowl and sniffed. "I think it's supposed to be stiffer, and I think I might have added a little too much of the stuff to make it smell nice, but . . . I'm sure it's fine."

Tracy grabbed Nora's arms. "Nora, Ms. Jacobs said — "

"I know. I know. But this is going to be a big hit. Wait and see."

Tracy followed Nora back to Ms. Nesbitt and watched, almost holding her breath, as Nora put the concoction on Ms. Nesbitt's hair. It hadn't been beaten enough, and instead of staying neatly on the customer's head, it began dripping down the sides of her face and onto her neck. Ms. Nesbitt reached up to dry her face and it dripped onto her arms. The strong smell of roses filled the room. Ms. Nesbitt shouted at Nora, "This stuff is awful. It's getting me all wet and it smells like a five-and-dime perfume. Get it off me."

Nora said condescendingly, "It's supposed to be on for ten minutes. Now you just relax and read a magazine." She handed the customer a magazine with hands that were dripping with the mousse.

"Get Margo," Ms. Nesbitt cried. "Immediately."

But Margo had heard the customer's outraged shouts and came running in. Tracy was already mopping Ms. Nesbitt's face. Margo took in the scene and asked, "Who did this?"

"It's just a little conditioner I made. What's all the excitement about?" Nora said.

"*You* made?" Margo said. "Are you some kind of nut?"

"Yes," Tracy whispered, and Nora glared at her.

The other customers in the room were getting upset and talking to each other. "What is wrong with this place, that Ms. Jacobs could let a thing like this happen?"

"Who is that strange child?"

"Keep her away from me."

Tracy ran from chair to chair talking quietly to the women, assuring them that Nora didn't mean any harm and wouldn't be doing anything like that again. They relaxed with her, and Nora watched in amazement. Tracy was a different person here, not at all the flaky girl her friends all thought she was.

When Ms. Nesbitt was ready to leave, she came over to Nora and smiled. "I know you didn't mean any harm and you thought you were doing the right thing, so why don't you just take this." She put the bill into Nora's hand. Nora was grinning inwardly, wishing she could see how much money she had in her hand, when Tracy came over.

She quickly opened Nora's hand, removed the bill, and returned it to Ms. Nesbitt. "Thank you so much, but Nora couldn't possibly take a tip."

"Wait," Nora said to Tracy, trying to get the bill back.

Tracy ignored Nora and smiled at Ms. Nesbitt. "I do hope you won't hold what happened against the Clip 'N' Curl."

"Of course not," Ms. Nesbitt replied. "But I am going to tell Tina Jacobs she should think of hiring you as a goodwill person . . . or something."

Just then a harried young man ran into the reception area and yelled at Margo. "She's not coming. She called me at the studio and told me she's not coming."

Margo held up a warning hand and said, "Calm down, Nick. Who's not coming?"

"Constanza, that's who. The woman isn't coming. What am I going to tell Ms. Jacobs?"

Margo closed her eyes wearily and then opened them. "*Who* is Constanza, and why should I care that she's not coming?"

Nick banged his hand on the reception desk and said, "Constanza is the model I use to take the pictures that are hanging all over the walls here. She models the latest hairdos. I guess we usually do the photos after the place is closed. But Ms. Jacobs is going to have a fit if I don't have new stuff for her this week."

"Well," Margo said, "you can't do what you can't do."

Tracy was listening, entranced, to all this. She took a deep breath and walked over to Nick. "I can do it."

"Do what?" Nick asked.

"I can model for your pictures. Look, I have long hair that you can do a million things with. And I'm pretty. Everyone says so."

"And modest, too," Nora mumbled.

Nick looked at Tracy carefully. "Have you ever modeled?"

Tracy shook her head. "No, but what's so hard? You just do my hair and take my picture."

"Stay here," Nick said to Tracy and left the room. He came back in a minute with a hairdresser. "Manuel," he said to the beautician, "can you do her hair in four new different ways?"

Manuel approached Tracy. "Turn," he ordered.

Slowly, Tracy turned in a full circle. Her eyes were wide and she was trying not to breathe hard.

Manuel picked up a strand of Tracy's long blonde hair and let it fall. "She has good hair, no doubt about that. I can fix her up. But how do you know she takes a decent picture?"

"I do, I do," Tracy said quickly. "Don't I, Nora?"

Nora said, "I've never seen — "

"See," Tracy interrupted, knowing Nora was going to say she had never seen anything but candid shots of Tracy. "See, Nora knows I take a wonderful picture."

Nick looked at Tracy suspiciously. "Okay, we'll give it a try, but don't think I'm going to pay you those fancy New York City prices. You're inexperienced and this is Cedar Groves."

"Of course, I don't expect that," Tracy said, having no idea what fancy New York City prices were.

"Okay, fifty dollars an hour, no more than that. And it should take a few hours to have your hair styled and to take the pictures. So it will be about one hundred and fifty dollars."

Nora and Tracy stared at each other and couldn't say a word. *One hundred and fifty dollars.*

"Let's start now," Nick said. "Manuel, do something with her hair, and I'll set up the camera and lights in one of the styling rooms."

Manuel took Tracy by the hand and said, "Come."

Nora was about to follow, when Margo said, "Don't you think you ought to hang around and do whatever you're supposed to do here?"

Nora looked at Tracy's retreating back with big, yearning eyes.

Margo sighed. "Oh, okay. On second thought you'll cause much less trouble watching Tracy. Go with her."

Nora grinned. "Thanks." And she ran after Tracy.

Manuel was in the process of combing Tracy's hair into a big soft knot on the top of her head, letting little tendrils fall onto her neck. Nora had never seen Tracy look as pretty. Manuel finished the styling by putting a red rose into the knot.

Nick came into the room and said, "Great. Come on kid, follow me."

Dutifully Nora and Tracy followed Nick into a room all done in soft peach. Nick's lights had been set up and he motioned for Tracy to sit in a chair. Then came an endless amount of time, adjusting the lights, putting makeup on, and Manuel rushing over to Tracy to fix a strand of hair here and there. Nick would then focus his camera on Tracy and bark orders, such as, "Look at me. Lower your chin. Wet your lips. Turn a little to the right. To the left."

After each order he would click his camera and yell, "Good. Perfect. Fine."

Manuel restyled Tracy's hair three times, and three times roll after roll of pictures were taken. In the middle of it, Margo came in. "The place is closing in ten minutes, but you can finish up anyway. Oh, and Ms. Jacobs called to say she was in the middle of baking a cake and wouldn't be back in time to close up. I told her everything was going great and not to worry about a thing."

"Why is she baking at a time like this?" Nick asked.

"She always bakes when she's in a panic. It's her way of releasing tension. The stuff always comes out rotten, but she doesn't know it."

At nine o'clock, Nick looked at Tracy and said, "Okay, we're through. Listen, kid, you were great. If you ever want to really model, let me know and I'll point you in the right direction."

Tracy got off the chair, rubbing her neck. "Thanks, Nick. But you know, modeling is sort of boring. I mean all I do is sit here and move my head around. And I have a stiff neck, too.

·I don't know if it's worth it. I'll have to think about it."

When Nora and Tracy left the beauty parlor, Nora looked at Tracy. "You have hidden depths. Did you know that?"

"Of course, I did," Tracy replied.

Chapter 12

Mitch knew there was going to be trouble as soon as he and Tommy walked into Norton's Sporting Goods. It was one of the largest stores in the mall and was on two floors. It hadn't occured to him before that it was going to be almost impossible to keep an eye on Tommy. Mitch just hoped Tommy would keep out of the way and not do anything disastrous.

Mr. Norton had already left when the boys arrived. There were four employees left in the big store, a salesperson for each floor and a cashier for each floor. One of the salesmen introduced himself to Mitch. "Hi, I'm Joe. Now just try to keep a low profile and let me and Bill do the selling. Bill is downstairs."

"Where's Mr. Norton?" Tommy asked.

Joe grinned. "He said he didn't want to stay

around to see you come in. He'd rather pretend this wasn't happening."

Mitch bristled. "Listen, Joe, I know a lot about sports. You don't have to worry about me."

"What about him?" Joe motioned to Tommy.

Mitch turned around to see that Tommy was already trying on a ski jacket and looking in the mirror to see how it fit. Mitch ran over to him and poked him. "What are you doing?"

"Looks pretty good on me, doesn't it?" Tommy said. "How much is it?"

"How do I know?" Mitch answered angrily.

Tommy shrugged. "You work here, don't you? I think you should know the price of the stuff."

"You work here, too," Mitch said. "Remember?"

"Oh, yeah," Tommy said. He took off the jacket and ran his comb through his hair. "Do I look okay?"

"Cut it out, Tommy," Mitch shouted.

Tommy looked over his shoulder at the store. "Listen, Mitch, keep your voice down, there are a lot of customers in here. I'll just go and see if I can help them."

Tommy walked over to a woman who was

examining a golf club. "Good-looking club, isn't it?" Tommy said. "It looks real good in your hands. Makes you look like a real golfer."

The woman peered at Tommy. "I *am* a real golfer. What are you, some kind of sexist?"

Tommy smiled and smoothed back his hair. "Me? No, sir. I love women."

"Aren't we lucky?" the customer said. "By the way, do you have any women salespeople here?"

"Women? Salespeople?" Tommy laughed out loud. "Well, this really isn't a field for women. You know what I mean."

"I know *exactly* what you mean," the woman said. She thrust the golf club into Tommy's hands. "Keep it." Then she started out of the store.

Mitch, who had been watching carefully, came running over. "Ma'am, what's the trouble? Would you like to see another club?"

"What I'd like to see is the outside of this store." She turned and looked at Tommy. "This young man should not be allowed in this place."

Tommy had a golf club in his hands. He had put a golf ball on the floor and swung wildly at the ball. By some accident, he hit it and it flew across the floor into a display of cans of tennis balls. The cans cascaded to the floor with a loud noise. Tommy looked at it with surprise.

Mitch shouted again. "What have you done? You turkey!"

Joe came running over and said, "What's going on here? Who made that mess? And whoever did, fix it. Now!"

"Fix it!" Mitch hissed at Tommy.

Hearing a commotion on the other end of the store, Mitch turned away from Tommy and gazed down the aisles. Five ten-year-old boys were happily throwing a baseball back and forth to each other. It flew between other customers in the store, who ducked to get out of the way.

"Hey, cut it out," Mitch yelled, but the boys ignored him. He raced over to the boys and tried running between them to catch the ball, but he never caught up with it.

Again, Joe came running. In one minute he had caught the ball and said to the boys, "Out! Now! Out!"

"Aw, Joe, come on," one of the boys yelled, but they left.

"I thought you said you were a sportsman," Joe said to Mitch.

"I am."

"So how come you couldn't catch a ball a bunch of ten-year-olds were tossing around?" Joe asked.

Before Mitch could answer, a man came over and said to him, "Can you please help me pick out a tennis racket? I'm just learning how to play and I'm not sure of what to buy."

Mitch paled slightly. He *was* good at sports and he *did* know a lot about them, but tennis wasn't one of the things he knew anything about. He could see Tommy nearby listening to every word and grinning. Tommy walked over and was about to talk to the man. Mitch knew that Tommy knew less than he did about tennis. He was getting ready to call Joe, much as he hated to, when three teenage girls came over to them.

One pretty, dark-haired girl said to the man, "Hi, my name is Clare, maybe I can help you. I play tennis a lot."

Clare and the other two girls totally ignored Mitch and Tommy, and soon they were showing the customer rackets and discussing the merits of each one. Then they moved on to another customer who was looking at skis.

Tommy looked at Mitch. "Are you going to let those girls take over? I mean, *girls* knowing more then you do?"

Mitch watched the girls and the customer who was listening carefully to whatever they were saying. "Well, they know what they're doing. And I could use the help, since you're none whatsoever."

"Now you've hurt my feelings," Tommy said, and he walked away.

The next hours were spent going from crisis to crisis. More kids came in and started pulling skis out of racks, trying on clothes, lighting flashlights, and trying to fill canteens at the water fountain. Mitch ran from group to group, trying to restore some kind of order to the store. Joe watched him and shook his head every now and then.

A man came in to return a baseball bat that was cracked, and when Mitch gently tried to find out if the bat had really been cracked before the man took it home, the man started yelling. "Are you calling me a liar?"

"No. No. Of course not," Mitch said desperately.

"Joe," the man called out. "Come over here. This kid said I was a liar."

Joe glared at Mitch. "Mr. Nearton is one of our best customers. If he said the bat was cracked . . . the bat was cracked."

"Sorry," Mitch grumbled. He looked around the store. Where was Tommy? He was nowhere in sight. Mitch wearily went down the stairs to the lower level, which was filled with customers, but there was no sign of Tommy. Mitch knew he couldn't shout for him in a crowded store, so he walked up and down the aisles, looking carefully for Tommy. He went past a camping tent that had been set up and some instinct made him look in. Tommy was curled up, asleep.

Mitch crawled in and shook Tommy's shoulder. "Wake up! You can't sleep here. You're supposed to be working."

Tommy sat up and rubbed his eyes. "Look, I'm just not very good at this. So I thought I'd just stay out of your way."

Mitch sat next to Tommy with his knees drawn up to his chest. He sighed. "You know, I learned something tonight. A person can be very good at some sports. Like a person could be good at basketball and football and swimming. But that doesn't mean a person is necessarily good at selling stuff. You know what I mean?"

Tommy nodded. "I know." Then he pulled out his comb and ran it through his hair.

Mitch narrowed his eyes, grabbed the comb, and threw it out of the tent. "Can you please go without combing your dumb hair for five minutes?"

Tommy was about to answer when a head

poked through the opening of the tent. Mr. Norton looked at the two boys. "Thanks for the sign. I was wondering where you were. Do you think you could come out now? It's eight o'clock."

Chapter 13

Jen ran into her house and slammed the door behind her. Ted Mann and Jeff Crawford were both in the living room reading, when Jen sped past them on her way to the stairs.

"Hey," her father called out. "How did it go?"

"Fine," Jen spat out. "Just fine!"

Mr. Mann came to the foot of the stairs and watched Jen as she ran up to her room. "Jen! What happened?"

Jen turned around and looked down at her father and at Jeff, who had joined him. "What happened? What happened is I found out that boys are awful. I don't want to talk about it, Dad. I'll see you in the morning."

Mr. Mann started up the stairs, but Jeff put a hand on his arm. "Don't. Let her alone until the morning. She won't say anything to you anyway."

Mr. Mann looked worried. "I guess you're right, but what do you think happened?"

"Something with Steve, I'm sure. I'd guess working together at the Burger Barn wasn't such a great idea."

Once in her room, Jen threw herself across the bed and dialed Nora's number. When she heard Nora's voice, Jen immediately said, "Steve is rotten, totally rotten!"

"Come on, Jen. Steve could never be rotten. What did he do?"

"He told me I was incompetent. He was arrogant and I never want to talk to him again."

Nora was amazed. "He said you were incompetent? That's ridiculous. Why did he say that?"

"Just because a kid had ketchup on her head, and . . ."

"*Why* did the child have ketchup on her head?" Nora interrupted.

Jen sighed. "It's too complicated, but I mean it, Nora, I am *through* with Steve. Probably with boys forever. Didn't life seem simpler before we were *really* interested in boys? Maybe we were better off. It was . . . well . . . more peaceful."

"I'm not really that involved with boys *now*. And I can tell you, peaceful or not, I wish I was."

"You date Brad, Nora. He's a boy," Jen said.

"Yeah," Nora answered. "But it's not like you and Steve. You know, real romance."

"Enough of boys," Jen said. "They aren't worth it. How did tonight work out for you and Tracy?"

Nora giggled. "It was fine for Tracy. You know, Jen, she is really quite together. She surprised me."

"*Tracy* is together?" Jen asked. "What about you?"

Nora hesitated. "Well, I sort of drowned a woman in a conditioning mousse."

"How could you do that? A mousse is thick."

"Well, mine wasn't," Nora said.

"Nora," Jen said, "you didn't make your own mousse, did you? You wouldn't do that to some unsuspecting woman?"

"I meant well," Nora said softly.

"You always *mean* well, Nora. You just don't learn . . . ever."

"I know. But Tracy saved the day — or night, rather. The woman loved *her*."

"I guess it wasn't such a great night for either one of us," Jen said.

"I certainly wouldn't want to do it again, but maybe the rest of the kids did okay."

"We'll find out tomorrow," Jen said.

* * *

The next day at lunchtime everyone pushed a few tables together, and they all sat down. Jen deliberately sat as far away from Steve as she could, and Andy sat a table away from Mia.

"Okay," Denise said. "Everyone should report on their night. I'll start. . . . I love clothes, but I'm certainly not very good at working in a boutique. But I think we made a nice amount of money. Didn't we, Lucy?"

"Pots," Lucy said. "And Denise is right. She's pretty dreadful working in a store. . . ."

"Gee, thanks," Denise muttered.

"Well, you said it first," Lucy answered. "Anyway, you didn't let me finish . . . but she would be great at buying stuff. So when we open a store, she'll buy and I'll manage."

"When are you opening a store?" Susan asked. "In a hundred years? And who is going to give you the money to open this great store?" Susan snickered.

Tommy threw his head back and laughed. "If there is one thing Denise doesn't have to worry about it's who's going to give her the money to do anything. You're dumb, Susan."

"Okay, smart one, how did *you* do?" Susan asked.

Tommy blushed. "Fine. Just fine. It was really quite . . . restful."

"Sure it was restful for you," Mitch scoffed.

"Because you went to sleep in a tent. A great help you were."

"You mean you stopped combing your hair long enough to go to sleep?" Jason said.

"So what happened to you, Jason?" Tommy asked. "I'll bet you were a disaster."

"There were a few minor mishaps, but I was okay. Now, Susan, of course, had problems."

"Me?" Susan yelled. "I'm not the one who did a skateboarding exhibition on the stage!"

"Yeah," Jason said, "but I'm not the one who was called a monster by an irate mother."

"Let's stop arguing," Lucy said. "How did you two do?" She turned to Andy and Mia.

"Oh, Mia is the expert," Andy said angrily. "She couldn't do anything wrong and as far as she was concerned, I couldn't do anything right."

"You didn't try hard enough," Mia said to Andy.

"See what I mean?" Andy said. "The expert."

"Well, there was more than *one* expert around last night," Jen said, not looking at Steve.

"We did okay, in spite of all these problems," Lucy said. "Does anyone know how much money we made?"

"I guess the owners will tell us tomorrow," Nora said. "I hope it paid off and was worth the agony."

"I didn't think it was agony," Tracy said. "I thought it was fun."

"That's because you were so good," Nora said.

"Tracy was *good*?" Susan said.

Tracy looked Susan right in the eye and said coolly and with confidence, "Yes, Susan, I was good."

Everyone around the table stared at the new Tracy, and they all burst into applause. Tracy stood up gracefully and bowed to her right and left.

After school, Jen walked home alone because Nora had a dentist's appointment. She was almost on her block, when she felt a hand on her arm. She knew right away whose hand it was. "I don't want to talk to you, Steve."

"Jennifer, please. I was wrong. I know it. But please listen."

"To what?" Jen asked, but she stopped walking.

"I was really a jerk," Steve said. "And rotten to you . . . and mean. But, I just wanted to impress you. You know, to show off to you, so you'd think I was . . . well, wonderful, I guess. I wanted you to think I knew everything about running a restaurant. I guess I let it all get out of hand."

"I think you're wonderful without knowing how to run a restaurant, Steve. Or at least, I used to think you were."

Steve put his arm around Jen's shoulders. "I'm sorry, Jen. Really. I'll never do anything like that again. Never put you down."

Jen looked down at the ground and then up at Steve. She reached up and put a hand on his cheek. "Okay. I forgive you . . . this once. But you can't be so macho anymore. It's dumb."

"I promise," Steve said, and he leaned over and kissed Jen's cheek. He looked up and down the empty block and then gently kissed her mouth.

Jeff, who was looking out of the window at them, said out loud, "Well, I guess they made up." He went to the phone and called Ted Mann. "Your daughter will be happier when you come home tonight. She and Steve have obviously cleared things up."

"How do you know?" Mr. Mann asked.

"I know because I'm a daring spy."

Mia walked by the record store and stood and stared in the window, thinking that this was where all the trouble with Andy had started. Was a Saturday job worth breaking up with Andy? But she knew it was more than the job. If Andy couldn't let her be the most she could be, then he couldn't really care much about her. Suddenly she was aware of the reflection of a boy with spiked hair and a leather collar around his neck in the store window. Mia looked at the boy in the window and said, "Hi."

"Hi," he said softly. "Want to go buy a record or something?"

Mia knew Andy wasn't the kind who could come right out and say he was sorry. But she had to know where he stood. She turned around and looked at him. "Sure. I'd like to buy a record or something. Would you like to buy one from me on Saturday . . . here?"

Andy smiled. "Sure. I'll be here . . . and then Saturday night you can take me to the movies with all the money you earn." His grin got bigger.

It was going to be okay. Mia knew that was what Andy was saying.

The next day the lead story in the *Cedar Groves Herald* was about the eighth grade in the mall. The headline was big and bold:

EIGHTH-GRADERS TAKE IN MORE THAN TWICE THE AMOUNT EXPECTED IN THE MALL

Cedar Groves: The eighth grade group astounded the store owners by raising more money for the pool than anyone thought they could. Last night is considered by all to have been a huge success, and Cedar Groves owes a big round of applause to these students who so competently did their jobs.

The article went on to list how much money was raised in each store, and quoted some of the owners' positive feelings about the night, including Mr. Yancy, who said, "Jennifer Mann and Steve Crowley, when faced with a crisis, came through. But I'm glad that night is over."

The eighth-graders all met at Temptations after school to celebrate. Once again they pushed four tables together and gathered around them.

"This is where it all began," Jen said dreamily.

"You know," Jason said, "maybe we could

think of a way to raise some more money."

Nora looked at him carefully, and then she picked up her glass of water and slowly poured it over Jason's head. "Jason," she said, "go soak your head."

Best friends, crushes, and lots of fun!

JUNIOR HIGH®
by Kate Kenyon

Join Nora, Jen, and the rest of the gang for lots of junior high madness and fun at Cedar Groves Junior High!

☐ 41497-6	#1	**Junior High Jitters**	$2.50
☐ 41649-9	#2	**Class Crush**	$2.50
☐ 41818-1	#3	**The Day the Eighth Grade Ran the School**	$2.50
☐ 40500-4	#4	**How Dumb Can You Get?**	$2.50
☐ 40899-2	#5	**Eighth Grade to the Rescue**	$2.50
☐ 41054-7	#6	**Eighth Grade Hero?**	$2.50
☐ 41160-8	#7	**Those Crazy Class Pictures**	$2.50
☐ 41161-6	#8	**Starring the Eighth Grade**	$2.50
☐ 41388-0	#9	**Who's the Junior High Hunk?**	$2.50
☐ 41389-9	#10	**The Big Date**	$2.50
☐ 41415-1	#11	**The Great Eighth Grade Switch**	$2.50
☐ 41788-6	#12	**The Revolt of the Eighth Grade**	$2.50
☐ 41787-8	#13	**Who's Haunting the Eighth Grade?**	$2.50
☐ 42028-3	#14	**Junior High Private Eyes**	$2.50
☐ 42029-1	#15	**The Night the Eighth Grade Ran the Mall** (April '89)	$2.50

PREFIX CODE 0-590-

Available wherever you buy books…or use the coupon below.

Scholastic Inc. P.O. Box 7502, 2932 E. McCarty Street
Jefferson City, MO 65102

Please send me the books I have checked above. I am enclosing $ _____
(please add $1.00 to cover shipping and handling). Send check or money order—no cash or C.O.D.'s please.

Name _____

Address _____

City_____ State/Zip_____

Please allow four to six weeks for delivery. Offer good in U.S.A. only. Sorry, mail order not available to residents of Canada. Prices subject to change.   JH988

SUNFIRE®

Read all about the fascinating young women who lived and loved during America's most turbulent times!

☐ 32774-7		**AMANDA** Candice F. Ransom	$2.95
☐ 33064-0		**SUSANNAH** Candice F. Ransom	$2.95
☐ 33156-6		**DANIELLE** Vivian Schurfranz	$2.95
☐ 33241-4	#5	**JOANNA** Jane Claypool Miner	$2.95
☐ 33242-2	#6	**JESSICA** Mary Francis Shura	$2.95
☐ 33239-2	#7	**CAROLINE** Willo Davis Roberts	$2.95
☐ 33688-6	#14	**CASSIE** Vivian Schurfranz	$2.95
☐ 33686-X	#15	**ROXANNE** Jane Claypool Miner	$2.95
☐ 41468-2	#16	**MEGAN** Vivian Schurfranz	$2.75
☐ 41438-0	#17	**SABRINA** Candice F. Ransom	$2.75
☐ 42134-4	#18	**VERONICA** Jane Claypool Miner	$2.75
☐ 40049-5	#19	**NICOLE** Candice F. Ransom	$2.25
☐ 42228-6	#20	**JULIE** Vivian Schurfranz	$2.75
☐ 40394-X	#21	**RACHEL** Vivian Schurfranz	$2.50
☐ 40395-8	#22	**COREY** Jane Claypool Miner	$2.50
☐ 40717-1	#23	**HEATHER** Vivian Schurfranz	$2.50
☐ 40716-3	#24	**GABRIELLE** Mary Francis Shura	$2.50
☐ 41000-8	#25	**MERRIE** Vivian Schurfranz	$2.75
☐ 41012-1	#26	**NORA** Jeffie Ross Gordon	$2.75
☐ 41191-8	#27	**MARGARET** Jane Claypool Miner	$2.75
☐ 41207-8	#28	**JOSIE** Vivian Schurfranz	$2.75
☐ 41416-X	#29	**DIANA** Mary Francis Shura	$2.75
☐ 42043-7	#30	**RENEE** Vivian Schurfranz (February '89)	$2.75

Scholastic Inc., P.O. Box 7502, 2932 East McCarty Street, Jefferson City, MO 65102

Please send me the books I have checked above. I am enclosing $ _____
(please add $1.00 to cover shipping and handling). Send check or money-order–no cash or
C.O.D.'s please.

Name _____

Address _____

City _____ State/Zip _____

Please allow four to six weeks for delivery. Offer good in U.S.A. only. Sorry, mail order not available
to residents of Canada. Prices subject to change.   **SUN 888**

A BEWITCHING NEW SERIES!

TEEN.™

Witch

NEW!

by Megan Barnes

Sarah Connell is not your typical teenager. She's a teen witch! And when Sarah tries to use her new powers, everything backfires with hilarious results! It's a fun comedy of errors that's sure to keep you laughing!

☐ 41296-5   #1 Lucky 13

☐ 41297-3   #2 Be Careful What You Wish For

☐ 41298-1   #3 Gone with the Witch

☐ 41299-X   #4 Witch Switch

$2.50 U.S./$3.50 CAN

Available wherever you buy books!

Scholastic Books